Outnumbering The Dead

OUTNUMBERING THE DEAD

Frederik Pohl

Illustrated by Steve Crisp

St. Martin's Press
New York

Library of Congress Cataloging-in-Publication Data

Pohl, Frederik.
    Outnumbering the dead / Frederick Pohl.
        p.   cm.
    ISBN 0-312-07755-6
    I. Title.
    PS3566.036094   1992
    813'.54—dc20   92-821
                                                                     CIP

First published in Great Britain by Random Century Group.

First U.S. Edition: May 1992
10 9 8 7 6 5 4 3 2 1

OUTNUMBERING
THE DEAD

1

Although the place is a hospital, or as much like a hospital as makes no difference, it doesn't smell like one. It certainly doesn't look like one. With the flowering vines climbing its walls and the soothing, gentle plink-tink *of the tiny waterfall at the head of the bed, it looks more like the de luxe suite in some old no-tell motel. Rafiel is now spruced up, replumbed and ready to go for another five years before he needs to come back to this place for more of the same, and so he doesn't look much like a hospital patient, either. He looks like a movie star, which he more or less is, who is maybe forty years old and has kept himself fit enough to pass for twenty-something. That part's wrong, though. After all the snipping and reaming and implanting they've done to him in the last eleven days, what he is is a* remarkably *fit man of ninety-two.*

When Rafiel began to wake from his designer dream he was very hungry (that was due to the eleven days he had been on intravenous feeding) and quite horny, too (that was the last of the designer dream). '*B'jour*, Rafiel,' said the soft, sweet voice of the nurser, intruding on his therapeutic dream as the last of it melted away. Rafiel felt the nurser's gentle touch removing the electrodes from his cheekbones, and, knowing very well just where he was and what he had been doing there, he opened his eyes.

He sat up in the bed, pushing away the nurser's velvety helping hand. While he was unconscious they had filled his room with flowers. There were great blankets of roses along one wall, bright red and yellow poppies on the windowsill that looked out on the deep interior court. '*Momento*, please,' he said to the nurser, and experimentally stretched his naked body. They had done a good job. That annoying little pain in the shoulder was gone and, when he held one hand before him, he saw that so were the age spots on his

7

skin. He was also pleased to find that he had awakened with a perfectly immense erection. 'Seems okay,' he said, satisfied.

'*Hai, claro*,' the nurser said. That was the server's programmed all-purpose response to the sorts of sense-free or irrelevant things hospital patients said when they first woke up. 'Your *amis* are waiting to come in.'

'They can wait.' Rafiel yawned, pleasantly remembering the last dream. Then, his tumescence subsiding, he slid his feet over the edge of the bed and stood up. He waved the nurser away and scowled in surprise. 'Shit. They didn't fix this little dizziness I've been having.'

'*Voulez* see your chart?' the nurser offered. But Rafiel didn't at all want to know what they'd done to him. He took an experimental step or two, and then the nurser would no longer be denied. Firmly it took his arm and helped him toward the sanitary room. It stood by as he used the toilet and joined him watchfully in the spray shower, the moisture rolling harmlessly down its metal flanks. As it dried him off, one of its hands caught his finger and held on for a moment – heartbeat, blood pressure, who knew what it was measuring? – before saying, 'You may leave whenever you like, Rafiel.'

'You're very kind,' Rafiel said, because it was his nature to be polite even to machines. To human beings too, of course. Especially to humans, as far as possible anyway, because humans were what became audiences and no sensible performer wanted to antagonize audiences. But with humans it was harder for Rafiel to be always polite, since his inner feelings, where all the resentments lay, were so frequently urging him to be the opposite – to be rude, insulting, even violent; to spit in some of these handsome young faces sometimes out of the anger that was always burning out of sight inside him. He had every right to that smouldering rage, since he was so terribly cheated in his life, but – he was a fair man – his special problem wasn't really their fault, was it? And besides, the human race in general had one trait that forgave them most others: they adored Rafiel. At least the surveys showed that 36.9 per

8

cent of them provably did, a rating which only a handful of utter superstars could ever hope to beat.

That sort of audience devotion imposed certain obligations on a performer. Appearance was one, and so Rafiel considered carefully before deciding what to wear for his release from the hospital. From the limited selection his hospital closet offered he chose red pantaloons, a luminous blue blouse and a silk cap to cover his unmade hair. On his feet he wore only moleskin slippers, but that was all right. He wouldn't be performing, and needed no more on the warm, soft, mossy flooring of his hospital room.

He time-stepped to the window, glancing out at the distant figures on the galleries of the hundred-metre atrium of the arcology he lived and worked in, and at the bright costumes of those strolling across the airy bridges, before he opaqued the window to study his reflection. That was satisfactory, though it would have been better if he'd had the closets in his condo to choose from. He was ready for the public who would be waiting for him – and for all the other things that would be waiting for him, too. He wondered how much time he had lost. He wondered if the redecoration of his condo had been completed, as it was supposed to have been while he was in the medical facility; he wondered if his agent had succeeded in re-booking the personal appearances he had had to miss, and whether the new show – what was it based on? Yes. *Oedipus Rex.* Whatever that was – had come together.

He was suddenly impatient to get on with his life, so he said, 'All right, they can come in now' – and a moment later, when the nurser had signalled the receptionists outside that it was all right, in they all came, his friends and colleagues from the new show: pale, tiny Docilia flying over to him with a quick kiss, Mosay, his dramaturge, bearing still more flowers, a corsage to go on Rafiel's blouse, Victorium with his music box hung around his neck, all grinning and welcoming him back to life. 'And *comment va* our Oedipus this morning?' Mosay asked, with pretend solicitude. Mosay didn't mean the solicitude to be taken seriously, of course, because there was really nothing for anyone to be solicitous

9

about. The nursers wouldn't have awakened Rafiel if all the work hadn't been successfully done.

'*Tutto bene*,' Rafiel answered as expected, letting Mosay press the bunch of little pink violets to his blouse and smelling their sweet scent appreciatively. 'Ready for work. Oh, and having *faim*, too.'

'But of course you are, after all *that*,' said Docilia, hugging him, 'and we have a lunch all set up for you. Can you go now?' she asked him, but looking at the nurser – which answered only by opening the door for them. Warmly clutching his arm and fondly chattering in his ear, Docilia led him out of the room where, for eleven days, he had lain unconscious while the doctors and the servers poked and cut and jabbed and mended him.

Rafiel didn't even look back as he entered this next serial instalment of his life. There wasn't any nostalgia in the place for him. He had seen it all too often before.

2

The restaurant – well, call it that; it is like a restaurant – is located in the midzone of the arcology. There are a hundred or so floors rising above it and a couple of hundred more below. It is a place where famous vid stars go to be seen, and so at the entrance to the restaurant there is a sort of tearoomy, saloony, cocktail-loungy place, inhabited by ordinary people who hope to catch a glimpse of the celebrities who have come there to be glimpsed. As Rafiel and his friends pass through this warm, dim chamber heads gratifyingly turn. Mosay whispers something humorous to Docilia and Docilia, smiling in return, then murmurs something affectionate to Rafiel, but actually all of them are listening more to the people around them than to each other. 'It's the short-time vid star,' one overheard voice says, and Rafiel can't help glowing a little at the recognition, though he would have preferred, of course, to have been a celebrity only for his work and not for his problem. 'I didn't know she was so tiny,' says another voice – speaking of Docilia, of course; they often say that. And, though Mosay affects not to hear, when someone says, 'He's got a grandissimo *coming up,* ils disent,' *his eyes twinkle a bit, knowing who that "he" is. But then the* maître d' *is coming over to guide them to their private table on an outside balcony.*

Rafiel was the last out the door. He paused to give a general smile and wink to the people inside, then stepped out into the warm, diffused light of the balcony, quite pleased with the way things were going. His friends had chosen the right place for his coming-out meal. If it was important to be seen going to their lunch, it was also important to have their own private balcony set aside to eat it on. They wanted to be seen while eating, of course, because every opportunity to be seen was important to theatre people – but from a proper distance. Such as on the balcony, where they were in view of all the people who chanced to be crossing the arcology atrium or looking out from the windows on the other side. The value of that was that then those people would say to the next persons they met, '*Senti*, guess who I saw at lunch today! Rafiel! And Docilia! And, *comme dit*, the music person.' And their names would be refreshed in the public mind one more time.

So, though this was to be an agendaed lunch, the balcony was the right place to have it. It wasn't a business-looking place; it could have been more appropriate for lovers, with the soft, warm breezes playing on them and hummingbirds hovering by their juice glasses in the hope of a hand-out. Really, it would have been more comfortable for a couple; for the four of them, with their servers moving between them with their buffet trays, it was a pretty tight squeeze.

Rafiel ravened over the food, taking great heaps of everything as fast as the servers could bring it. His friends conspired to help. 'Give him *pommes*,' Mosay ordered, and Docilia whispered, 'Try the *sushi ceveche*, it's *fine*.' Mouth full and chewing, Rafiel let his friends fuss over him. From time to time he raised his eyes from his food to smile at jest or light line, but there was no need for him to take part in the talk. He was just out of hospital, after all. (As well as being a star, even among these stars; but that was a given.) He knew that they would get down to business quickly enough. Docilia was always in a hurry to get on with the next production and Mosay, the dramaturge – was, well, a dramaturge. It was his *business* to get things moving. Meanwhile, it was Rafiel's right to satisfy one appetite and to begin to plan ahead for the pleasing prospect of relieving the other. When Docilia put a morsel of pickled fish between his lips he licked her fingertips affectionately and looked into her eyes.

He was beginning to feel at ease.

The eleven days in the medical facility had passed like a single night for Rafiel, since he had been peacefully unconscious for almost all of it. He saw, though, that time had passed for the others, because they had changed a little. Mosay was wearing a little waxed moustache now and

12

Victorium was unexpectedly deeply tanned, right up to his *cache-sexe* and on the expanse of belly revealed by his short embroidered vest. Docilia had become pale blonde again. For that reason she was dressed all in white, or almost all: white bell-bottomed pants and a white halter top that showed her pale skin. The only touch of contrast was a patch of fuzzy peach-coloured embroidery at the crotch of the slacks that, Rafiel was nearly sure he remembered, accurately matched the outlines of her pubic hair. It was a very Docilia kind of touch, Rafiel thought.

Of course, they were all very smartly dressed. They always were; like Rafiel they owed it to their public. The difference between Rafiel and the others was that every one of them looked to be about twenty years old – well, ageless, really, but certainly, at the most, no more than a beautifully fit thirtyish. They always had looked that way. All of them did. All ten *trillion* of them did, all over the world and the other worlds, or anyway nearly all. . . . Except, of course, for the handful of oddities like himself.

When Docilia saw Rafiel's gaze lingering on her – observing it at once, because Docilia was never unaware when someone was looking at her – she reached over and fondly patted his arm. He leaned to her ear to pop the question: '*Bitte*, are you free this afternoon?'

She gave him a tender smile. 'For you,' she said, almost sounding as though she meant it, '*siempre*.' She picked up his hand and kissed the tip of his middle finger to show she was sincere. '*Mais* can we talk a little business first? Victorium's finished the score, and it's *belle*. We've got—'

'Can we play it over *casa tu*?'

Another melting smile. '*Hai*, we can. *Hai*, we will, as much as you like. But, listen, we've got a wonderful second-act duet, you and I. I love it, Rafiel! It's when you've just found out that the woman you've been shtupping, that's me, is your mother, that's me, too. Then I'm telling you that what you've done is a sin . . . and then at the end of the duet I run off to hang myself. Then you've got a solo dance. Play it for him, Victorium?'

Victorium didn't need to be begged; a touch of his fingers

on his amulet recorder and the music began to pour out. Rafiel paused with his spoon in his juicy white sapote fruit to listen, not having much choice. It was a quick, tricky jazz tune coming out of Victorium's box, but with blues notes in it too, and a funny little hoppety-skippy syncopation to the rhythm that sounded Scottish to Rafiel.

'*Che? Che?*' Victorium asked anxiously as he saw the look on Rafiel's face. 'Don't you like it?'

Rafiel said, 'It's just that it sounds – gammy. *Pas* smooth. Sort of like a little limp in there.'

'*Hai! Precisamente!*' cried Mosay. 'You caught it at once!'

Rafiel blinked at him. 'What did I catch?'

'What Victorium's music conveyed, of course! You're playing Oedipus Rex and he's *supposed* to be lame.'

'Oh, *claro*,' said Rafiel; but it wasn't really all that clear to him. He wiped the juice of the sapote off his lips while he thought it over. Then he asked the dramaturge, 'Do you think it's a good idea for me to be dancing the part of somebody who's lame?' He got the answer when he heard Docilia's tiny giggle, and saw Victorium trying to smother one of his own. 'Ah, *merde*,' Rafiel grumbled as, once again, he confronted the unwelcome fact that it was not his talent but his oddity that delighted his audiences. Ageing had been slowed down for him, but it hadn't stopped. His reflexes were not those of a twenty-year-old; and it was precisely those amusing little occasional stumbles and slips that made him *Rafiel*. 'I don't like it,' he complained, knowing that didn't matter.

'But you *must* do it that way,' cried the dramaturge, persuasive, forceful – being a dramaturge, in short, with a star to cajole into shape. '*C'est toi*, really! The part could have been made for you. Oedipus has a bit of a physical problem, but we see how he rises above his limitations and dances beautifully. As, always, do yourself, Rafiel!'

'*D'accord*,' Rafiel said, surrendering as he knew he must. He ate the fruit for a moment, thinking. When it was finished he pushed the shell aside and asked sourly, 'How lame is this Oedipus supposed to be, exactly?'

'He's a *blessé*, a little bit. He has something wrong with his ankles. They were mutilated when he was a baby.'

'Hum,' said Rafiel, and gave Victorium a nod. The musician replayed the five bars of music.

'Can you dance to it?' Victorium asked anxiously.

'Of course I can. If I had my tap shoes—'

'Give him his tap shoes, Mosay,' Docilia ordered, and then bent to help Rafiel slip them on, while the dramaturge clapped his hands for a server to bring a tap mat.

'Play from the end of the duet,' Rafiel ordered, abandoning his meal to stand up in the narrow space of the balcony. He moved slightly, rocking back and forth, then began to tap, not on the beat of the music, but just off it – *step left, shuffle right* – while his friends nodded approvingly – *spank it back, scuff it forward*. But there wasn't really enough room. One foot caught another; he stumbled and almost fell, Victorium's strong hand catching him. 'I'm clumsier than ever,' he sighed resentfully.

'They'll love it,' Mosay said, reassuring him, and not lying, either, Rafiel knew unhappily; for what was it but his occasional misstep, the odd quaver in his voice – to be frank about it, the peculiarly fascinating traits of his advancing age – that made him a superstar?

He finished his meal. 'Come on, Docilia. I'm ready to go,' he said, and although the others clearly wanted to stay and talk they all agreed that what Rafiel suggested was a good idea. They always did. It was one of the things that made Rafiel's life special – one of the good things. It came with being a superstar. He was used to being indulged by these people, because they needed him more than he needed them, although, as they all knew, they were going to live for ever and he was not.

3

*All the worlds know the name of Rafiel, but, actually, 'Rafiel'
isn't all of his name. That name, in full, is Rafiel Gutmaker-
Fensterborn, just as Docilia, in full, is Docilia Megareth-Morb,
and Mosay is Mosay Koi Mosayus. But 'Rafiel' is all he needs.
Basically, that is the way you can tell when you've finally become
a major vid star. You no longer need all those names to be
identified or even to get your mail delivered. Even among a race
of ten trillion separate, living, named human beings, when you
have their kind of stardom a single name is quite enough.*

Rafiel's difficulty at present was that he didn't happen to
be in his own condo, where his mail was. Instead he was
in Docilia's, located fifty-odd storeys above his own in the
arcology. He really did want to know what messages were
waiting for him.

On the other hand, this particular delay was worthwhile.
Although Rafiel had been sleeping for eleven days, his
glands had not. He was well charged up for the exertions
of Docilia's bed. He came to climax in record time – the
first time – with Docilia helpfully speeding him along. The
second time was companionably hers. Then they lay pleasantly spooned, with Rafiel drowsily remembering now and
then to kiss the back of her neck under the fair hair. It
wasn't Alegretta's hair, he thought, though without any real
pain (you couldn't actually go on aching all your life for a
lost love, though sometimes he thought he was coming
close); but it was nice hair, and it was always nice to make
love to this tiny, active little body. But after a bit she stretched, yawned and left him, fondly promising to be quickly
back, while she went to return her calls. He rolled over to
gaze at the pleasing sight of her naked and youthfully sweet
departing back.

It was a fact, Rafiel knew, that Docilia wasn't youthful in

any chronological sense. In terms of life span she was certainly a good deal older than himself, however she looked. But you couldn't ignore the way she looked, either, because the way she looked was what the audiences were going to see. As the story of *Oedipus Rex* began to come back to him, he began to wonder: Would any audience believe for one moment that this girlish woman could be his mother?

It was a silly thought. The audiences weren't going to worry about that sort of thing. If it registered with them at all it would be only another incongruity of the kind that they loved so well. Rafiel dismissed the worry, and then, as he lay there, pleasantly at ease, he at last became aware of the faint whisper of music from Docilia's sound system.

So it had been an agendaed tryst after all, he thought tolerantly. But a sweet one. If she had not forgotten to have Victorium's score playing from the moment they entered her flat, at least she had been quite serious about the lovemaking he had come there for. So Rafiel did what she wanted him to do; he lay there, letting the music tell its story to his ears. It wasn't a bad score at all, he thought critically. He was beginning to catch the rhythms in his throat and feet when Docilia came back.

She was glowing. 'Oh, Rafiel,' she cried, '*look* at this!'

She was waving a tomograph, and when she handed it to him he was astonished to see that it was an image of what looked like a three-month foetus. He blinked at her in surprise. 'Yours?'

She nodded ecstatically. 'They just sent it from the creche,' she explained, nervous with pleasure. 'Isn't it *très belle*?'

'Why, that's *molto bene*,' he said warmly. 'I didn't know you were *enceinte* at all. Who's the *padre*?'

She shrugged prettily. 'Oh, his name is Charlus. I don't think you know him, but he's really good, isn't he? I mean, *look* at that gorgeous child.'

In Rafiel's opinion no first-trimester foetus could be called anything like 'gorgeous', but he knew what was expected of him and was not willing to dampen her delight.

17

'It's certainly a good-looking embryo, *senza dubito*,' he told her with sincerity.

'His *always* are! He's fathered some of the best children I've ever seen – good-looking, and with his dark blue eyes, and oh, so tall and strong!' She hesitated for a moment, prettily almost blushing. Then, 'We're going to share the *bambino* for a year,' she confided proudly. 'As a family, I mean. When the baby's born Charlus and I are going to start a home together. Don't you think that's a wonderful idea?'

There was only one possible answer to that. 'Of course I do,' said Rafiel, regardless of whether he did or not.

She gave him a fond pat. 'That's what you ought to do too, Rafiel. Have a child with some nice *dama*, bring the baby up together.'

'And when would I find the time?' he asked. But that wasn't a true answer. The true answer was that, yes, he would have liked nothing better, provided the right woman was willing to donate the ovum . . . but the right woman had, long ago, firmly foreclosed that possibility.

Docilia had said something that he missed. When he asked for a repeat, she said, 'I said, and it'll help my performance, won't it?'

He was puzzled. 'Help how?'

She said, impatient with his lack of understanding, 'Because Jocasta's a *mutter*, don't you see? That's the whole point of the story, isn't it? And now I can get right into the part, because I'm being a *mutter*, too.'

Rafiel said sincerely, 'You'll be fine.' He meant it, too. He had assumed she would all along.

'Yes, *certo*,' she said absently, thinking already of something else. 'I think I ought to give a copy to the dad. He'll be so excited.'

'*I* would be,' Rafiel agreed. She blinked and returned her attention to him. She lifted the sheet and peered under it for a thoughtful moment.

'I think,' she said judiciously, 'if you're not in a great hurry to leave, if we just give it a few more minutes. . . . '

'No hurry at all,' he said, pulling her down to him and

stroking her back in a no-hurry-at-all way. 'Well,' he said. 'So what else have you been doing? Did they release your *Inquisitor* yet?'

'Three days ago,' she said, rubbing her foot along his ankle. 'God, those clothes were so *heavy*, and then the last scene — You didn't see it, of course?'

'How could I?'

'No, of course not. Well, try to, *si c'est* possible, because I'm really fine in the *auto-da-fé* scene.'

'What scene?' Rafiel knew that Docilia had finished shooting something about the Spanish Inquisition, with lots of torture – torture stories always went well in this world that had so little personal experience of any kind of suffering. But he hadn't actually seen any part of it.

'Where they burn me at the stake. *Quelle horreur!* See, they spread the wood all around in a huge circle and light it at the edges, and I'm chained to the stake in the middle. *Che cosa!* I'm running from side to side, trying to get away from the fire as it burns toward me, and then I start burning myself, *capisce?* And then I just fall down on the burning coals.'

'It sounds wonderful,' Rafiel said, faintly envious. Maybe it was time for him to start looking for dramatic parts instead of all the song and dance?

'*I* was wonderful,' she said absently, reaching under the covers to see what was happening. Then she turned her face to his. 'And, guess what? You're getting to be kind of wonderful yourself, *galubka*, right now. . . . '

Three times was as far as Rafiel really thought he wanted to go. Anyway, Docilia was now in a hurry to send off the picture of her child. 'Let yourself out?' she asked, getting up. Then, naked at her bedroom door, she stopped to look back at him.

'We'll all be fine in this *Oedipus*, Rafiel,' she assured him. 'You and me in the lead parts, and Mosay putting it all together, and that *merveilleux* score.' Which was still repeating itself from her sound system, he discovered.

20

He blew her a kiss, laughing. 'I'm listening, I'm listening,' he assured her. And did in fact listen for a few moments.

Yes, Rafiel told himself, it really was a good score. *Oedipus* would be a successful production, and when they had rehearsed it and revised it and performed it and recorded it, it would be flashed all over the solar system, over all Earth and the Moon and the capsule colonies on Mars and Triton and half a dozen other moons, and the orbiting habitats wherever they might be, and even to the distant voyagers well on their way to some other star – to all ten million million human beings, or as many of them as cared to watch it. And it would *last*. Recordings of it would survive for centuries, to be taken out and enjoyed by people not yet born, because anything that Rafiel appeared in became an instant classic.

Rafiel got up off Docilia's warm, shuddery bed and stood before her mirror, examining himself. Everything the mirror displayed looked quite all right. The belly was flat, the skin clear, the eyes bright – he looked as good as any hale and well-kept man of middle years would have looked, in the historically remote days when middle age could be distinguished from any other age. That was what those periodical visits to the hospital did for him. Though they couldn't make him immortal, like everyone else, they could at least do *that* much for his appearance and his general comity.

He sighed and rescued the red pantaloons from the floor. As he began to pull them on he thought: They can do all that, but they could not make him live for ever, like everyone else.

That wasn't an immediate threat. Rafiel was quite confident that he would live a while yet – well, quite a *long* while, if you measured it in days and seconds, perhaps another thirty years or so. But then he wouldn't live after that. And Docilia and Mosay and Victorium – yes, and lost Alegretta, too, and everyone else he had ever known – would perhaps take out the record of this new *Oedipus Rex* now and then and look at it and say to each other, 'Oh, do you remember dear old Rafiel? How sweet he was. And what a pity.' But dear old Rafiel would be *dead*.

21

4

The arcology Rafiel lives and works in rises 235 storeys above central Indiana, and it has a population of 165,000 people. That's about average. From outside – apart from its size – the arcology looks more like something you'd find in a kitchen than a monolithic community. You might think of it as resembling the kind of utensil you would use to ream the juice out of an orange half (well, an orange half that had been stretched long and skinny), with its star-shaped cross section and its rounding taper to the top. Most of the dwelling units are in the outer ribs of the arcology's star. That gives a tenant a nice view, if he is the kind of person who really wants to look out on central Indiana. Rafiel isn't. As soon as he could afford it he moved to the more expensive inside condos overlooking the lively central atrium of the arcology, with all its glorious light and its graceful loops of flowering lianas and its wall-to-wall people – people on the crosswalks, people on their own balconies, even tiny, distant people moving about the floor level nearly two hundred storeys below. To see all that is to see life. From the outer apartments, what can you see? Only farmlands, and the radiating troughs of the maglev trains, punctuated by the to-the-horizon stretch of all the other arcologies that rose from the plain like the stubble of a monster beard.

In spite of all Rafiel's assurances, Docilia insisted on getting dressed and escorting him back to his own place. She chattered all the way. 'So this city you saved, *si chiama* Thebes,' she was explaining to him as they got into the elevator, 'was in a *hell* of a mess before you got there. Before Oedipus did, I mean. This Sphinx creature was just making *schrecklichkeit*. It was doing all kinds of rotten things – I don't know – like killing people, stealing their food, that sort of thing. I guess. Anyway, the whole city was just *desperate* for help, and then you came along to save them.'

22

'And I killed the Sphinx, so they made me *roi de* Thebes out of gratitude?'

'*Certo!* Well, almost. You see, you don't have to *kill* it, exactly. It has this riddle that no one can figure out. You just have to solve its riddle, and then it I guess just goes kaput. So then you're their hero, Oedipus, but they don't exactly make you king. The way you get to be that is you marry the queen. That's me, Jocasta. I'm just a *pauvre petite* widow lady from the old dead king, but as soon as you marry me that makes you the *capo di tutti capi*. I'm still the queen, and I've got a brother, Cleon, who's a kind of a king, too. But you're the boss.' The elevator stopped, making her blink in slight surprise. 'Oh, *siamo qui*,' she announced, and led the way out of the car.

Rafiel halted her with a hand on her shoulder. 'I can find my way home from here. You didn't need to come with me at all, *verstehen sie?*'

'I wanted to, *piccina*. I thought you might be a little, well, wobbly.'

'I am wobbly, all right,' he said, grinning, '*mais pas* from being in the hospital.' He kissed her, and then turned her around to face the elevator. Before he released her he said, 'Oh, listen. What's this riddle of the Sphinx I'm supposed to solve?'

She gave him an apologetic smile over her shoulder. 'It's kind of dopey. "What goes on four legs, two legs and three legs, and is strongest on two." Can you imagine?'

He looked at her. 'You mean you don't know the answer to that one?'

'Oh, but I do know the answer, Rafiel. Mosay told me what it was. It's—'

'Go on, Cele,' he said bitterly. '*Auf wiedersehen.* The answer to that riddle is "a man", but I can see why it would be hard for somebody like you to figure it out.'

Because, of course, he thought as he entered the lobby of his condo, none of these eternally youthful ones would ever experience the tottery, 'three-legged', ancient-with-a-cane phase of life.

*

23

'Welcome back, Rafiel,' someone called, and Rafiel saw for the first time that the lobby was full of paparazzi. They were buzzing at him in mild irritation, a little annoyed because they had missed him at the hospital, but nevertheless resigned to waiting on the forgivable whim of a superstar.

It was one of the things that Rafiel had had to resign himself to, long ago. It was a considerable nuisance. On the other hand, to be truthful, it didn't take much resignation. When the paps were lurking around for you, it proved your fame, and it was always nice to have renewed proof of that. He gave them a smile for the cameras, and a quick cut-and-point couple of steps of a jig – it was a number from his biggest success, the *Here's Hamlet!* of two years earlier. 'Yes,' he said, answering all their questions at once, 'I'm out of the hospital, I'm back in shape, and I'm hot to trot on the new show that Mosay's putting together for me, *Oedipus Rex.*' He started toward the door of his own flat. A woman put herself in his way.

'Raysia,' she introduced herself, as though one name were enough for her, too. 'I'm here for the interview.'

He stopped dead. Then he recognized the face. Yes, one name was enough, for a top pap with her own syndicate. 'Raysia, dear! *Cosi bella* to see you here, but – what interview are we talking about?'

'Your dramaturge set the appointment up last week,' she explained. And, of course, that being so, there was nothing for Rafiel to do but to go through with it, making a mental note to get back to Mosay at the first opportunity to complain at not having been told.

But giving an interview was not a hard thing to do, after all, not with all the practice Rafiel had had. He fixed the woman up with a drink and a comfortable chair and took his place at the exercise barre in his study – he always liked to be working when he was interviewed, to remind them he was a dancer. First, though, he had a question. It might not have occurred to him if Docilia hadn't made him think of lost Alegretta, but now he had to ask it. He took a careful

24

first position at the barre and swept one arm gracefully aloft as he asked, 'Does your syndicate go to Mars?'

'Of course. I'm into *toutes les biosphères*,' she said proudly, 'not just Mars, but Mercury and the moons and nearly every orbiter. As well as, naturally, the whole planet Earth.'

'That's wonderful,' he said, intending to flatter her and doing his best to sound as though this sort of thing hadn't ever happened to him before. Slowly, carefully, he did his barre work, hands always graceful, getting full extension on the legs, her camera following automatically as he answered her questions. Yes, he felt fine. Yes, they were going to get into production on the new *Oedipus* right away – yes, he'd heard the score, and yes, he thought it was wonderful. 'And the playwright,' he explained, 'is the greatest writer who ever lived. Wonderful old Sophocles, two thousand nearly seven hundred years old, and the play's as fresh as anything today.'

She looked at him with a touch of admiration for an actor who had done his homework. 'Have you read it?'

He hadn't done *that* much homework, though he fully intended to. 'Well, not in the original,' he admitted, since a non-truth was better than a lie.

'I have,' she said absently, thinking about her next question – disconcertingly, too. Rafiel turned around at the barre to work on the right leg for a while. Hiding the sudden, familiar flash of resentment.

'*Vous êtes* terrible,' he chuckled, allowing only rueful amusement to show. 'All of you! You *know* so much.' For they all did, and how unfair. Imagine! This child – this ancient twenty-year-old – reading a Greek play in the original, and not even Greek, he thought savagely, but whatever rough dialect had been spoken nearly three thousand years ago.

'*Mais pourquoi non?* We have time,' she said, and got to her question. 'How do you feel about the end of the play?' she asked.

'Where Oedipus blinds himself, you mean?' he tried, doing his best to sort out what he had been told of the

25

story. 'Yes, that's pretty bloody, isn't it? Stabbing out his own eyes, that's a very powerful—'

She was shaking her head. 'No, *pas du tout*, I don't mean the blinding scene. I mean at the very end, where the chorus says' – her voice changed as she quoted –

> See proud Oedipus!
> He proves that no mortal
> Can ever be known to be happy
> Until he is allowed to leave this life,
> Until he is dead,
> And cannot suffer any more.

She paused, fixing him with her eye while the camera zeroed in to catch every fleeting shade of expression on his face. 'I'm not a very good translator,' she apologized, 'but do you feel that way, Rafiel? I mean, as a mortal?'

Actors grow reflexes for situations like that – for the times when a fellow player forgets a line, or there's a disturbance from the audience – when something goes *wrong* and everybody's looking at you and you have to deal with it. He dealt with it. He gave her a sober smile and opened his mouth. '*Hai*, that's so true, in a way,' he heard his mouth saying. '*N'est ce pas?* I mean, not just for me but, *credo*, for all of us? It doesn't matter however long we live, there's always that big final question at the end that we call "death", and all we have to confront it with is courage. And that's the lesson of the story, I think: courage! To face all our pains and fears and go on anyway!'

It wasn't good, he thought, but it was enough. Raysia shut off her camera, thanked him, asked for an autograph and left; and as soon as the door was closed behind her Rafiel was grimly on the phone.

But Mosay wasn't answering, had shut himself off. Rafiel left him a scorching message and sat down, with a drink in his hand, to go through his mail. He was not happy. He scrolled quickly through the easy part – requests for autographs, requests for personal appearances, requests for interviews. He didn't have to do anything about most of them; he rerouted them through Mosay's office and they would be dealt with there.

A note from a woman named Hillaree could not be handled in that way. She was a dramaturge herself – had he ever heard of her? He couldn't be sure; there were thousands of them, though few as celebrated as Mosay. Still, she had a proposition for Rafiel. She wanted to talk to him about a 'wonderful' (she said) new script. The story took place on one of the orbiting space habitats, a place called *Hakluyt*, and she was, she said, convinced that Rafiel would be determined to do it, if only he would read the script.

Rafiel thought for a moment. He wasn't convinced at all. Still, on consideration, he copied the script to file without looking at it. Perhaps he would read the script, perhaps he wouldn't; but he could imagine that, in some future conversation with Mosay, it might be useful to be able to mention this other offer.

He sent a curt message to this Hillaree to tell her to contact his agent and then, fretful, stopped the scroll. He wasn't concentrating. Raysia's interview had bothered him. 'We have time' indeed! Of course they did. They had endless time, time to learn a dead language, just for the fun of it, as Rafiel himself might waste an afternoon trying to learn how to bowl or paraglide at some beach. They *all* had time – all but Rafiel himself and a handful of other unfortunates like him – and it wasn't fair!

It did not occur to Rafiel that he had already had, in the nine decades since his birth, more lifetime than almost anyone in the long history of the human race before him. That was irrelevant. However much he had, everyone around him had so much *more*.

Still, in his ninety years of life Rafiel had learned a great deal – even actors could learn more than their lines, with enough time to do it in. He had learned to accept the fact that he was going to die, while everyone he knew lived on after him. He had even learned why this was so.

27

It was all a matter of the failings of the Darwinian evolution process.

In one sense, Darwinian evolution was one of the nicest things that had ever happened to life on Earth. In the selection of desirable traits to pass on to descendants – the famous 'survival of the fittest' – virtue was rewarded. Traits that worked well for the organism were passed on, because the creatures that had them were more likely to reproduce than the ones lacking them.

Over the billions of years the process had produced such neat things – out of the unpromising single-celled creatures that began it all – as eyes, and anuses, and resistance to the diseases that other organisms wanted to give you, and ultimately even intelligence. That was the best development, in the rather parochial collective opinion of the intelligent human race. Smarts had turned out to be an evolutionary plus; that was why there were ten trillion human beings around, and hardly any of such things as the blue whale, the mountain gorilla and the elephant.

But there was one thing seriously wrong with the way the process works. From the point of view of the individual organism itself, evolution doesn't do a thing. Its benefits may be wonderful for the *next* generation, but it doesn't do diddly-squat for the organisms it is busily selecting, except to encourage the weaker ones to die before they get around to reproducing themselves.

That means that some very desirable traits that every human being would have liked to have – say, resistance to osteoporosis, or a wrinkle-free face – didn't get selected for in the Darwinian lottery. Longevity was not a survival feature. Once a person (or any other kind of animal) had its babies, the process switched itself off. Anything that benefited the organism after it was finished with its years of reproducing was a matter of pure chance. However desirable the new trait might have been, it wasn't passed on. Once the individual had passed the age of bearing young, the Darwinian score-keepers lost interest.

That didn't stop such desirable traits from popping up. Mutations appeared a million times which, if passed on,

would have kept the lucky inheritors of subsequent generations hale for indefinite periods – avoiding, let us say, such
inconveniences of age as going deaf at sixty, incontinent at
eighty and mindless by the age of a hundred. But such
genes came and went and were lost. As they didn't have
anything to do with reproductive efficiency, they didn't get
preserved. There wasn't any selective pass-through after
the last babies were born.

So longevity was a do-it-yourself industry. There was no
help from Darwin. But. . . .

But once molecular biology got itself well organized, there
were things that *could* be done. And were done. For most
of the human population. But now and then, there were an
unfortunate flawed few who missed out on the wonders of
modern life-prolonging science because some undetectable
and incurable quirks in their systems rejected the necessary
treatment. . . .

Like Rafiel. Who scrolled through, without actually
seeing, the scores of trivial messages – fan letters, requests
for him to appear at some charitable function in some
impossible place, bank statements, bills – that had arrived
for him while he was away. And then, still fretful, turned
off his communications and blanked his entertainment
screen and even switched off the music as, out of habit and
need, he practised his leaps and entrechats in the solitude
of his home, while he wondered bitterly what the point was
in having a life at all, when you knew that it would sooner
or later *end*.

5

People do still die now and then. It isn't just the unfortunates like Rafiel who do it, either, though of course they are the ones for whom it is inevitable. Even normal *people sometimes die as well. They die of accident, of suicide, of murder, sometimes just of some previously unknown sickness or even of a medical blunder that crashes the system. The normal people simply do not do that very often. Normal people expect to live normally extended lives. How long those lives can be expected to last is hard to say, because even the oldest persons around aren't yet much more than bicentenarians (that's the time since the procedures first became available), and they show no signs of old age yet. And, of course, since people do go on giving birth to other people, all that longevity has added up to quite an unprecedented population explosion. The total number of human beings living today is something over ten trillion – that's a one followed by thirteen zeroes – which is far more than the total number of previous members of the genus* Homo *in every generation since the first Neanderthalers appeared. Now the living overwhelmingly outnumber the dead.*

When Rafiel woke the next morning he found his good nature had begun to return. Partly it was the lingering wisps of his last designer dream – Alegretta had starred in it, as ordered, and that lost and cherished love of his life had never been more desirable and more desiring, for that matter, because that was the kind of a dream he had specified. So he woke up in a haze of tender reminiscence. Anyway, even the terminally mortal can't dwell on their approaching demise all the time, and Rafiel was naturally a cheerful man.

Getting out of bed in the morning was a cheerful occasion, too, for he was surrounded with the many, many things he had to be cheerful about. As he breakfasted on what the servers brought him he turned on the vid tank and watched half a dozen tapes of himself in some of the highlights of his career. He was, he realized, quite good. In the tank his miniature self sang love ballads and jiving patter numbers and even arias, and his dancing – well, yes, now and then a bit trembly, he conceded to himself, but with *style* – was a delight to watch. Even for the person who had done it, but who, looking in the tank, could only see that imaged person as a separate and, really, very talented entity.

Cheerfully Rafiel moved to the barre to begin his morning warm-ups. He started gently, because he was still digesting his breakfast. There wasn't any urgency about it. Rehearsal call was more than an hour away, and he was contentedly aware that the person he had been looking at on the vid was a *star*.

In a world where the living far outnumbered the dead, space was precious. On the other hand, so was Rafiel, and stars were meant to be coddled. Mosay had taken a rehearsal room the size of a tennis court for Rafiel's own private use. The hall was high up in the arcology, and it wasn't just a big room. It was a very well-equipped one. It had bare powder-blue walls that would turn into any colour Rafiel wanted them to be at the touch of a switch, a polished floor of real hardwood that clacked precisely to his taps, and, of course, full sound and light projection. Mosay, fussing over his star's accommodations, touched the keypad, and the obedient projectors transformed the bare walls into a glittering throne room.

'I'm afraid that it's the wrong period, of course,' Mosay apologized, looking without pleasure at the palace of Versailles, 'no *roi soleil* in Thebes, is there, but I want you to get the feel of the kingship thing, *sapete*? We don't have the programs for the Theban backdrops yet. Actually I don't know if we will, because as far as my research people can tell, the Thebans really didn't have any actual thronerooms anyway.'

'It doesn't matter,' Rafiel said absently, slipping into his tap shoes.

'It does to me! You know how I am about authenticity.'

31

Seeing what Rafiel was doing Mosay hastily turned to touch the control keys again. Victorium's overture began to tinkle from the hidden sound system. *'C'est beau, le son?* It's just a synthesizer arrangement so far.'

'It's fine,' said Rafiel.

'Are you sure? Well, *bon*. Now, *bitte*, do you want to think about how you want to do the first big scene? That's the one where you're onstage with all the townspeople. They'll be the chorus. You're waiting to find out what news your brother-in-law, Creon, has brought back from the Delphic oracle; he went to find out what you had to do to get things straightened out in Thebes. . . . '

'I've read the script, of course,' said Rafiel, who had in fact finished scrolling through it at breakfast.

'Of course you have,' said Mosay, rebuked. 'So I'll let you alone while you try working out the scene, shall I? Because I want to start checking out shooting locations tomorrow, and so I've got a million things to do today.'

'Go and do them,' Rafiel bade him. When the dramaturge was gone Rafiel lifted his voice and commanded: 'Display text, scene one, from the top. With music.'

The tinkling began again at once, and so did the display of the lines. The words marched along the upper parts of the walls, all four walls at once so that wherever Rafiel turned he saw them. He didn't want to dance at this point, he thought. Perhaps just march back and forth – yes, remembering that the character was lame – yes, and a king too, all the same. . . . He began to pantomime the action and whisper the words of his part:

CHORUS: Ecco Creon, crowned with laurels.

'He's going to say,' Rafiel half-sang in his turn, 'what's wrong's our morals.'

[*Enter* CREON.]
CREON: *D'accord*, but I've still worse to follow.
It's not me speaking. It's Apollo.

Rafiel stopped the crawl there and thought for a second.

32

There were some doubts in his mind. How well was that superstitious mumbo-jumbo going to work? You couldn't expect a modern audience to take seriously some mumble from a priestess. On the other hand, and equally of course, Oedipus had not been a modern figure. Would *he* have taken it seriously? Yes, Rafiel decided, he had to, or else the story made no sense to begin with. In playing Oedipus, then, the most he could do was to show a little tolerant exasperation at the oracle's nagging. So he started the accompaniment again, and mimed a touch of amused patience at Creon's line, turning his head away—

And caught a glimpse of an intruder watching him rehearse from the doorway.

It was a small, unkempt-looking young man in a lavender kilt. He was definitely not anyone Rafiel had seen as a member of Mosay's troupe and therefore no one who had a right to be here. Rafiel gave him a cold stare and decided to ignore him.

He realized he'd missed a couple of Creon's lines, and his own response was coming up. He sang:

OEDIPUS: We'll take care of all this hubble-bubble as
Soon as you tell us what the real trouble is.

But his concentration was gone. He clapped his hands to stop the music and turned to scowl at the intruder.

Who advanced to meet him, saying seriously, 'I hope I'm not interfering. But on that line—'

Rafiel held up a forbidding hand. 'Who are you?'

'Oh, sorry. I'm Charlus, your choreographer. Mosay said—'

'I do my own choreography!'

'Of course you do, Rafiel,' the man said patiently. 'You're *Rafiel*. I shouldn't have said choreographer, when all Mosay asked me to do was be your assistant. Do you remember me? From when you did *Make Mine Mars*, twenty years ago it must have been, and I tried out for the chorus line?'

Then Rafiel did identify him, but not from twenty years ago. 'You sired Docilia's little one.'

33

Charlus looked proud. 'She told you, then? *Evvero*. We're both so happy – but, look, maestro, let me make a suggestion on that bubble-as, trouble-is bit. Suppose. . . . '

And the man became Oedipus on the spot, as he performed a simultaneous obscene gesture and courtly bow, ending on one knee.

Rafiel pursed his lips, considering. It was an okay step. No, he admitted justly, it was more than that. It wasn't just an okay step, it was an okay *Rafiel* step, with just a little of Rafiel's well-known off-balance stagger as the right knee bumped the floor.

He made up his mind. '*Khorashaw*,' he said. 'I don't usually work with anybody else, but I'm willing to give it a try.'

'*Spasibo*, Rafiel,' the man said humbly.

'*De nada*. Have you got any ideas about the next line?'

Charlus looked embarrassed. '*Hai*, sure but *est-ce* possible to go back a little bit, to where you come in?'

'My first entrance, at the beginning of the scene?'

Charlus nodded eagerly. 'Right there, *pensez-vous* we might try something real macho? You are a king, after all – and you can enter like. . . . '

He turned and repeated Oedipus's entrance to the hall, but slowly, s-l-o-w-l-y, with his head rocking and a ritual-istic, high-stepping strut and turn before he descended sedately to a knee again. It was the same finish as the other step, but a world different in style and meaning.

Rafiel pursed his lips. 'I like it,' he said, meditating, 'but do you think it really looks, well, Theban? I'd say it's *peut-être* basically Asian – maybe Thai?'

Charlus looked at him with new respect. 'Close enough. It's *meno o mino* the Javanese *patjak-kulu* movement. Am I getting too eclectic for you?'

Rafiel acknowledged, 'Well, I guess I'm pretty eclectic myself.'

'I know,' said Charlus, smiling.

While Charlus was showing the mincing little *gedruk* step

34

he thought would be good for Jocasta, Mosay looked in, eyebrows elevated in the obvious question.

Charlus was tactful. 'I've got to make a trip to the *benjo*,' he said, and Rafiel answered the unspoken question as soon as the choreographer was gone.

'Mind his helping out? No, I don't mind, Mosay. He's no performer himself, but as a choreographer, *hai*, he's *good*.' Rafiel was just. The man was not only good, he was bursting with ideas. Better still, it was evident that he had watched every show Rafiel had ever done, and knew Rafiel's style better than Rafiel did himself.

'*Bene, bene*,' Mosay said with absent-minded satisfaction. 'When you hire the best people you get the best results. Oh, and *senti*, Rafiel' – remembering, as he was already moving toward the door – 'those messages you forwarded to me? A couple of them were personal, so I routed them back to your machine. They'll be waiting for you. *Continuez, mes enfants*.' And a pat on the head for the returning Charlus and the dramaturge was gone, and they started again.

It was hard work, good work, with Rafiel happy with the way it was going, but long work, too; they barely stopped to eat a couple of sandwiches for lunch, and even then, though not actually dancing, Rafiel and Charlus were working with the formatting screen, moving computer-generated stick figures about in steps and groupings for the dance numbers of the show, Rafiel getting up every now and then to try a step, Charlus showing an arm gesture or a bob of the head to finish off a point.

By late afternoon Rafiel could see that Charlus was getting tired, but he himself was going strong. He had forgotten his hospital stay and was beginning to remember the satisfactions of collaboration. Having a second person help him find insights into the character and action was a great pleasure, particularly when that person was as unthreatening as the eager and submissive Charlus. 'So now,' Rafiel said, towelling some sweat away, 'we're up to where we've found out that Thebes won't get straight until the assassin of the old king is found and punished, right? And this is where I sing my vow to the gods—'

'*Permesso?*' Charlus said politely. And took up a self-important strut, half tap, almost cakewalk, swinging his lavender kilt as he sang the lines: 'I swear, without deceit or bias, We'll croak the rat who croaked King Laius.'

'Yes?' said Rafiel, reserving judgment.

'And then Creon gives you the bad news. He tells you that, *corpo di bacco*, things are bad. The oracle says that the murderer is here in Thebes. I think right there is when you register the first suspicion that there's something funny going on. You know? Like . . . ' miming someone suddenly struck by an unwanted thought.

'You don't think that's too early?'

'It's what you think that counts, Rafiel,' Charlus said submissively, and looked up toward the door.

Mosay and Docilia were looking in, the dramaturge with a benign smile, Docilia with a quick kiss for Rafiel and another for Charlus. Although their appearance was a distraction, the kiss turned it into the kind of distraction that starts a new and pleasing line of thought; Docilia was in white again, but a minimum of white: a short white wraparound skirt, a short wraparound bolero on top, with bare flesh between and evidently nothing at all underneath. 'Everything going all right?' the dramaturge asked, and answered himself: 'Of course it is; it's going to be a *merveille du monde*. Dear ones, I just stopped by to tell you that I'm leaving you for a few days; I'm off to scout out some locations for shooting.'

Rafiel took his eyes off Docilia and blinked at him. 'We're going to make *Oedipus* on location?'

'I insist,' said Mosay firmly. 'No *faux* backgrounds; I want the real thing for *Oedipus*! We're going to have a Thebes that even the Thebans would admire, if there were any of them left.'

Charlus cleared his throat. 'Is Docilia going with you?' he asked.

That question had not occurred to Rafiel to ask, but once it was asked he wanted to know the answer, too. Mosay was looking thoughtfully at the choreographer. 'Well,' he said,

'I thought she might have some ideas. . . . Why do you want to know that?'

Charlus had an answer ready. 'Because we've started to work out some of the *pas de deux* routines, and Docilia ought to have a chance to try them out.' Rafiel did not think it was a truthful one.

Evidently Mosay didn't, either. He pursed his lips, considering, but Docilia answered for him. 'Of course I should,' she said. 'You go on without me, Mosay. Have a nice trip; I'll see you when you get back. Only please, dear, try to find a place that isn't too *hot*. I sweat so when I'm dancing, you know.'

Whatever plans Charlus had for Docilia, they were postponed. When at last they were through rehearsing, Docilia kissed the choreographer absently and pulled Rafiel along with her out of the room before Charlus could speak. '*J'ai molto faim*, dear,' she said – but only to Rafiel, 'and I've booked a table for us.'

In the elevator, Rafiel looked at her thoughtfully. 'Didn't Charlus want to see you?'

She smiled up at him, shrugging. 'But he acted as though he didn't want you to go off with Mosay,' Rafiel persisted. 'Or with me either, for that matter. Is he, well, jealous?'

'Oh, Rafiel! What a terrible word that is, "jealous". Are you thinking of, what, the Othello thing?'

'He's the father of your child,' Rafiel pointed out uncomfortably.

'*Mais oui*, but why should he be jealous if I'm shtupping you or Mosay, *liebling*? I shtup him too, whenever he likes – when I don't have another date, of course. Come and eat a nice dinner, and stop *worrying*.'

They walked together to their table – not on a balcony this time, but on a kind of elevated dais at the side of the room, so they could be well seen. It was the kind of place where theatre people gathered, at the bottom of the atrium. Tables in the open surrounded the fiftieth-floor rooftop lake. There was a net overhead to catch any carelessly dropped objects, and from time to time they could hear the whine of the magnets pulling some bit of trash away. But nothing ever struck the diners. The place was full of children, and Docilia smiled at every one of them, practising her upcoming motherhood. And swans floated in the lake, and stars were woven into the net overhead.

When the servers were bringing their monkey-orange juice Rafiel remembered. 'Speaking of Charlus. He had an idea for your scene at the end. You know? Just before you go to hang yourself? As you're going out. . . . '

He looked around to see who was looking at them, then decided to give the fans a treat. He stood up and, in the little cleared space between their table and the railing, did the step Charlus had called '*gedruk*', mincing and swaying his hips. It was not unnoticed. Soft chuckles sounded from around the dining room. 'Oh, maybe yes,' Docilia said, nodding, pleased. 'It gets a laugh, doesn't it?'

'Yes,' said Rafiel, 'but that's the thing. Do we want *comedy* here? I mean, you're just about to die. . . . '

'Exactly, dear,' she said, not understanding. 'That's why it will be twice as funny in the performance.'

'*Aber* a *morceau* incongruous, don't you think? Comedy and death?'

She was more puzzled than ever. '*Hai*, that's what's funny, isn't it? I mean, *dying*. That's such a bizarre thing, it always makes the audience laugh.' And then, when she saw his face, she bit her lip. '*Pas* all that funny for everybody, is it?' she said remorsefully. 'You're so *normal*, dear Rafiel. Sometimes I just forget.'

He shrugged and forgave her. 'You know more about that than I do,' he admitted, knowing that he sounded still grumpy – glad when a famous news comic came over to chat. Being the kind of place it was, table-hopping was, of course, compulsory. As pleased as Rafiel at the interruption, Docilia showed her tomographs of the baby to the comic and got the required words of praise.

Then it was Rafiel's turn to blunder. 'What sort of surrogate are you using?' he asked, to make conversation, and she gave him a sharp look.

'Did somebody tell you? No? Well, it's cow,' she said,

and waited to see what his response would be. She seemed aggrieved. When all he did was nod non-committally, she said, 'Charlus wanted to use something fancier. Do you think I did the right thing, Rafiel? Insisting on an ordinary cow surrogate, I mean? So many people are using water buffalo now. . . . '

He laughed at her. 'I wouldn't know, would I? I've never been a parent.'

'Well, I have and, believe me, Rafiel, it isn't easy. What *difference* does it make, really, what kind of animal incubates your child for you? But Charlus says it's important and, oh, Rafiel, we had such a battle over it!'

She shook her head, mourning the obstinacy and foolishness of men. Then she decided to forgive. 'It isn't altogether his fault, I suppose. He's worried. Especially now. Especially because it's almost *fin* the second trimester and that means it's time—'

She came to a quick halt, once more biting her lip. Rafiel knew why: it was more suddenly remembered tact. The end of the second trimester was when they had to do the procedure to make the child immortal, because at that point the foetal immune system wasn't developed yet and they could manipulate it in the ways that would make it live essentially for ever.

'That's a scary time, I know,' said Rafiel, to be comforting, but of course he did know. Everyone knew he knew, and why he knew. The operation was serious for a little foetus. A lot of them died, when the procedure didn't work – or managed to survive, but with their natural immune systems mortally intact. Like Rafiel.

'Oh, *mon cher*,' she said, 'you know I didn't mean anything *personal* by that!'

'Of course you didn't,' he said reassuringly; but all the same, the happy buzz of the day's good rehearsing was lost, the evening's edge was gone, and long before they had finished their leisurely supper, he had abandoned any plan of inviting her back to his condo for the night.

It did spoil the evening for him. Too early for sleep, too

late to make any other arrangements, he wandered alone through his condo. He tried reading, but it seemed like a lot of effort. He glanced toward the bar, but his muscles were sore enough already from the day's work-out. He switched on the vid, roaming the channels to see if there was anything new and good, but there wasn't. A football series coming to its end in Katmandu, an election in Uruguay – who cared about such things? He paused over a story about a habitat now being fitted out with engines to leave the solar system: it was the one named *Hakluyt* and it held his interest for a moment because of that silly woman, Hillaree, with her script. It would be interesting, he thought, to take that final outward leap to another star . . . Of course, not for him, who would be long dead before the expedition could hope to arrive. He switched to the obituaries – his favourite kind of news – but the sparse list held no names that interested him. He switched again to the entertainment channels. There was a new situation comedy that he had heard about. The name was *Dachau*, and he remembered that one of the parts was played by a woman he had slept with a few times, years ago. Now she was playing a – a what? – a concentration-camp guard in Germany in World War II, it seemed. It was a comic part; she was a figure of fun as the Jews and Gypsies and political enemies who were inmates constantly mocked and outwitted her. It did have its funny bits. Rafiel laughed as one of the inmates, having escaped to perform some heroic espionage feat for the Allies, was sneaked back into the camp under the very eyes of the commandant. Still, he wondered if things had really ever been that *jolly* in the real concentration camps of the time, where the real death ovens burned all day and all night.

It all depended on whether you were personally involved, he thought.

And then he switched it off, thinking of Docilia. He shouldn't have been so curt with her. She couldn't help being what she was. If death seemed comical to the deathless, was that her fault? Hadn't most of the world, for centuries on end, found fun in the antics of the dwarves and the deformed, even making them jesters at their courts? Perhaps the hunchbacks themselves hadn't found anything to laugh at – but that was *their* point of view.

As his attitude toward dying was his own.

He thought for a moment of calling Docilia to apologize – perhaps the evening might be salvaged yet. Then he remembered what Mosay had said about personal messages and scrolled them up.

The first one was personal, all right, and a surprise. It was a talking message, and as soon as the picture cleared he recognized the face of the man who happened to have been his biological father.

The man hadn't changed a bit. (Well, why would he, in a mere ninety-some years?) He was as youthful and as handsome as he had been when, on a rare visit, he had somewhat awkwardly taken young Rafiel on his knee. 'I saw you were in the *krankhaus* again,' the man in the screen said, with the look of someone who was paying a duty call on an ailing friend – not a close one, though. 'It reminded me we haven't heard from each other in a long time. I'm glad everything *fait bon*, Rafiel – son – and, really, you and I ought to have lunch together some *prossimo giorno.*'

That was it. Rafiel froze the picture before it disappeared, to study the dark, well-formed face of the man whose genes he had carried. But the person behind the face eluded him. He sighed, shrugged and turned to the other message. . . .

And that one made him stiffen in his chair, with astonishment too sharp to be joy.

It wasn't an imaged message, or even a spoken one; it was a faxed note, in a crabbed, nearly illegible handwriting that he knew very well:

Dearest Rafiel, I was so glad to hear you got through another siege with the damned doctors. *Mazeltov.* I'm sending you a little gift to celebrate your recovery – and to remind you of me, because I think of you so very often.

What the gift was he could not guess, because it hadn't

41

arrived yet, but the note was signed, most wonderfully signed:

For always, your Alegretta.

6

Naturally, all kinds of connections and antipathies appear among the Oedipus troupe as they come together. Charlus is the sire of Docilia's unborn child. Andrev, who is to play the Creon, is the son of the composer of the score, Victorium. Ormeld, the Priest, and Andrev haven't acted together for thirty-five years, because of a nasty little firefight over billing in what happened to be the first production in which either got an acting credit. (They hug each other with effusive but wary joy when they come together in the rehearsal hall.) Sander, the Tiresias, studied acting under Mosay when Mosay had just abandoned his own dramatic career (having just discovered how satisfying the god-behind-the-scenes role of a dramaturge was). Sander is still just a little awed by his former teacher. All these interconnections are quite separate from the ordinary who-had-been-sleeping-with-whom sort of thing. They had to be kept that way. If people dragged up that sort of ancient history they'd never get everything straight. Actually, nobody is dragging anything up – at least, not as far as the surface where it can be seen. On the contrary. Everybody is being overtly amiable to everybody else and conspicuously consecrated to the show, so far. True, they haven't yet had much chance to be anything else, since it's only the first day of full-cast rehearsal.

Although Mosay was still off scouting for locations – somewhere in *Turkey*, somebody said, though why anybody would want to go to *Turkey* no one could imagine – he had taken time to talk to them all by grid on the first day. 'Line up, everybody,' he ordered, watching them through the monitor over his camera. 'What I want you to do is just a quick run-through of the lines. Don't sing. Don't dance, don't even act – we just want to say the words and see each other. Docilia, please leave Charlus alone for a minute and pay attention. Victorium will proctor for me, while I' – a small but conspicuous sigh; Mosay had not forgotten his acting skills – 'keep trying to find the *right* location for our production.'

Actually it was Rafiel who was paying least attention, because his mind was full of lost Alegretta. Now, perhaps, found again? For you never forgot your first love. . . .

Well, yes, you did, sometimes, but Rafiel never had. Never could have, in spite of the sixty or seventy – could it have been eighty? a hundred? – other women he had loved, or at least made love to, in the years since then. Alegretta had been something very special in his life.

He was twenty years old then, a bright young certain-to-be-a-star song and dance man. Audiences didn't know that yet, because he was still doing the kind of thing you had to start out with, cheap simulations and interactives, where you never got to make your own dramatic *statement*. The trade was beginning to know him, though, and Rafiel was quite content to be working his way up in the positive knowledge that the big break was sure to come. (And it had come, no more than a year later.)

But just then he had, of all things, become sick. (No one got *sick*!) When the racking cough began to spoil his lines, he had to do something. He complained to his doctors about it. Somewhat startled (people didn't *have* coughs), the doctors put him in a clinic for observation, because they were as discomfited by it as Rafiel himself. And when all the tests were over, the head resident herself came to his hospital room to break the bad news.

Even all these decades later, Rafiel remembered exactly what she had looked like that morning. Striking. Sexy, too; he had noticed that right away, in spite of the circumstances. A tall woman, taller in fact than Rafiel himself; with reddish-brown hair, a nose with a bit of a bend in it that kept it from being perfect in any orthodox way, but a smile that made up for it all. He had looked at her, made suspicious by the smile, a little hostile because a little scared. She sat down next to him, no longer smiling. 'Rafiel,' she said directly, 'I have some bad news for you.'

'*Che c'e?* Can't you fix this damn cold?' he said, irritated.

She hesitated before she answered. 'Oh, yes, we can cure

44

that. We'll have it all cleared up by morning. But you see, you shouldn't have a cough at all now. It means. . . . ' She paused, obviously in some pain. 'It means the procedure didn't work for you,' she said at last, and that was how Alegretta told Rafiel that he was doomed to die in no more than another hundred years, at most.

When he understood what she was saying, he listened quietly and patiently to all the explanations that went with it. Queerly, he felt sorrier for her than for himself – just then he did, anyway; later on, when it had all sunk in, it was different. But as she was telling him that such failures were very rare, but still they came up now and then, and at least he had survived the attempt, which many unborn babies did not, he interrupted her. 'I don't think you should be a doctor,' he told her, searching her lovely face.

'Why not?' she asked.

'You take it too hard. You can't stand giving bad news.'

She said soberly, 'I haven't had much practice at it, have I?'

He laughed at her. She looked at him in surprise; but then, he was still in his twenties, and a promise of another hundred years seemed close enough to forever. 'Practise on me,' he urged. 'When I'm released, let's have dinner.'

They did. They had a dozen dinners, those first weeks, and breakfasts too, because that same night he moved into her flat above the hospital wing. They stayed together nearly two weeks; and there had never been another woman like her. 'I'll never tell,' she promised when they parted. 'It's a medical confidence, you know. A secret.' She never had told, either.

And his career did blossom. In those days Rafiel didn't need to be an oddity to be a star, he became a star because he was so damn good.

It was only later on that he became an oddity as well because, though Alegretta had never told, there were a lot of other checkups, and ultimately somebody else had.

It had not mattered to Rafiel, then, that Alegretta was nearly a hundred to his twenty. Why should it? Such things made no difference in a world of eternal youth. Alegretta did not look one minute older than himself. . . . And it was only later, when she had left him, and he was miserably trying to figure out why, that he realized the meaning of the fact that she never would.

First run-throughs didn't matter much. All they were really for was to get the whole cast together, to get some idea of their lines and what the relationship of each character was to the others, who was what to whom. They didn't act, much less sing; they read their lines at half-voice, eyes on the prompter scroll on the wall more than each other. It didn't matter that Rafiel's mind was elsewhere. When others were onstage he took out the fax from Alegretta and read it again. And again. But he wasn't, he thought, any more inattentive than any of the others. The pretty young Antigone – what was her real name? Bruta? Something like that – was a real amateur, and amateurishly she kept trying to move toward stage front each time she spoke. Which was not often; and didn't matter, really, because when Mosay came back he would take charge of that sort of thing in his gentle, irresistible way. And Andrev, the Creon, had obviously never even looked at the script, while Sander, who was to play the blind prophet, Tiresias, complained that there wasn't any point in doing all this without the actual dramaturge being present. Victorium had his hands full.

But he was dealing with it. When they had finished the quick run-through he dispatched Charlus to start on the choreography of the first scene, where all the Thebans were reciting for the audience their opening misery under the Sphinx. Rafiel was reaching in his pocket for another look at the fax when Victorium came over. '*Sind sie* okay, Rafiel?' he asked. 'I thought you seemed just a little absent-minded.'

'*Pas du tout*,' Rafiel said, stuffing the letter away. Then, admitting it, 'Well, just a little, *forse*. I, ah, had a letter from an old friend.'

'Yes,' Victorium said, nodding, 'Mosay said something about it. Alegretta, was that her name?'

Rafiel shrugged, not letting his annoyance show. Of

course Mosay had known all about Alegretta, because Mosay made it a point to know everything there was to know about every one of his artists; but to pry into private mail, and then to discuss it with others, was going too far.

'Old lovers can still make the heart beat faster, can't they?' he said.

'Yes?' Victorium said, not meaning to sound sceptical, but obviously not troubled with any such emotions himself. 'Has it been a long time? Will you be seeing her again?'

'Oh' – startled by the thought, almost afraid of it – 'no, I don't think so. No, probably not – she's a long way away. She seems to be in one of the orbiters now. You know she used to be a doctor? But now she's given up medicine, doing some kind of science now.'

'She sounds like a very interesting person,' Victorium said neutrally – a little absent-mindedly himself, too, because in the centre of the room Charlus had started showing the Thebans the dance parts, and Victorium had not failed to catch the sounds of his own music. Still looking at the Thebans, Victorium said, 'Mosay asked me to show you the rough simulation for the opening. Let's go over to the small screen – oh, hell,' he said, interrupting himself, 'can you *pardonnez-moi* a minute? *Verdammt*, Charlus has got them *hopping* when the music's obviously *con vivace*. I'll be right back.'

Rafiel listened to the raised voices, giving them his full willed attention in order to avoid a repetition of the rush of feeling that Victorium's casual suggestion had provoked. Charlus seemed to be winning the argument, he thought, though the results would not be final until Mosay returned to ratify them. It was a fairly important scene. Antigone, Ismene, Polyneices and Eteocles – the four children of Oedipus and Jocasta – were doing a sort of *pas de quatre* in tap, arms linked like the cygnets in *Swan Lake*, while they sang a recapitulation of how Oedipus came and saved them from the horrid Sphinx. The chorus was being a real chorus, in fact a chorus line, tapping in the background and, one by one, speaking up – a potter, a weaver, a soldier, a house-hold slave – saying yes, but things are going badly now and something must be *done*. Then Rafiel would make his entrance as Oedipus and the story would roll on . . . but not today.

Victorium was breathing hard when he rejoined Rafiel. 'You can ignore all that,' he said grimly, 'because I'm sure Mosay isn't going to let that *dummkopf* dance-teacher screw up the *grand ensemble*. Never mind.' He snapped on the prompter monitor to show what he and Mosay had programmed for the under-the-credits opening. 'Let's get down your part here. This is before the actual story begins, showing you and the Sphinx.'

Rafiel gave it dutiful attention. Even in preliminary stick-figure simulation, he saw that the monster on the screen was particularly unpleasant-looking, like a winged reptile. '*Che* the hell *cosa* is that?'

'It's the Sphinx, of course. What else would it be?' Victorium said, stopping the computer simulation so Rafiel could study the creature.

'It doesn't look like a sphinx to me. It looks like a crocodile.'

'Mosay,' Victorium said with satisfaction, 'looked it up. Thebes was a city on the Nile, you know. The Nile is *famous* for crocodiles. They sacrificed people to them.'

'But this one has wings.'

'*Perchè no?* You're probably thinking of that other Egyptian sphinx. The old one out of the desert? This one's different. It's a *Theban* sphinx, and it looks like whatever Mosay says it looks like.' Victorium gave him the look of someone who would like to chide an actor for wasting time with irrelevant details – if the actor hadn't happened to be the star of the show. 'The important thing is that it was terrorizing the whole city of Thebes, after their *ancien roi*, Laius, got murdered, until you came along and got rid of it for them. Which, of course, is why the Thebans let you marry Jocasta and be their *nouveau roi*.' He thought for a moment. 'I'll have to write some new music for the Sphinx to sing the riddle, but,' he said wistfully, 'Mosay says we don't want too much song and dance here because, see, *tutti qui* is just a kind of prologue. It isn't in the Sophocles

48

play. We'll just run it under the credits to mise the scene
– oh, *merde*. What's that?'

He was looking at the tel window on the screen, where
Rafiel's name had begun to flash.

'Somebody's calling me, I guess,' Rafiel said.

'You shouldn't be getting personal calls during rehearsal,
should you?' he chided. Then he shrugged. '*San ferian*. See
who it is, will you?'

But when Rafiel tapped out his acceptance no picture
appeared on the screen, just a voice. It wasn't even the
voice of a 'who'. It was the serene, impersonal voice of his
household server, and it said:

'A living organism has been delivered for you. It is a gift.
I have no program for caring for living creatures. Please
instruct me.'

'Now who in the world,' Rafiel marvelled, 'would be
sending me a *pet*?'

It wasn't anyone in the world – not the planet Earth, anyway;
as soon as Rafiel saw the note pinned to the cage, where
the snow-white kitten purred contentedly inside, he knew
who it was from.

This is my favourite cat's best kitten, dear Rafiel. I hope
you'll love it as much as I do.

Rafiel found himself laughing out loud. How strange of
Alegretta. How dear, too! Imagine anyone keeping a *pet*. It
was not the kind of thing immortals were likely to do. Who
wanted to get attached to some living thing that was sure
to die in only a few years – only a moment, in the long
lifetime of people now alive? (Most of them, anyway.) But
it was a sweet thought, and a sweet little kitten, he found
as he uneasily picked it up out of the cage and set it on his
lap. The pretty little thing seemed comfortable there, still
purring as it looked up at him out of sleepy blue eyes.

Most important, it was a gift from Alegretta. He was
smiling as, careful not to disturb the little animal, he began

searching his data bases for instructions on the care and feeding of kittens.

7

*Rafiel has decided not to make love to Docilia again. He isn't
sure why. He suspects it has something to do with the fact
that the sire of her child is always nearby, which makes him
uncomfortable. It isn't just that they've collaborated on creating
a foetus that makes him shy off, it is more the fact that they
intend to be a family. It is only later that he realizes that that
means he can't bed any of the other members of the troupe, either.
Not the Antigone, the little girl named Bruta, though she has
asked him to – not even though she happens to have interested
him at first, since she has auburn hair and her nose is not
perfectly straight. (Perhaps it is because she looks a little bit like
Alegretta that he especially doesn't want to make love to her.)
Not any of them, in spite of the fact that, all through his performing life, Rafiel has seldom failed to make love in person to every
female he was required to make love to in the performance, on the
principle that it added realism to his art. (He wasn't particularly
attracted to most of those women, either, only prepared to make
sacrifices for his art.) This time, no. The only sensible reason
he can give himself for this decision is that Docilia would surely
find out, and it would hurt her feelings to be passed over for the
others.*

None of this inordinate chastity was because he didn't desire
sexual intercourse. On the contrary. He didn't need to
program designer dreams of love-making. His subconscious
did all the programming he needed. Almost every morning
he woke from dreams of hot and sweaty quick encounters
and dreamily long-drawn-out ones. The root of the problem
was that, although he wanted to do it, he didn't want to do
it *with* anyone he knew. (One possible exception always
noted, but always inaccessible.) So he slept alone. When,
one morning, some slight noise woke him with the scent of
perfumed woman in his nose he supposed it was a lingering

dream. Then he opened his eyes. A woman was there, in his room, standing by a chair and just stepping out of the last of her clothing. 'Who the hell are you?' he shouted as he sat up.

The woman was quite naked and entirely composed. She sat on the edge of his bed and said, 'I'm Hillaree. You looked so sexy there, I thought I might as well just climb in.'

'How the hell did you get into my condo?'

'I'm a dramaturge,' she said simply. 'How much would you respect me if I let your doorwarden keep me out?'

Rafiel turned in the bed to look at her better. She was a curly-headed little thing, with a wide, serious mouth, and he was quite sure he had never seen her before.

But he had heard her name, he realized. 'Oh, *that* dramaturge,' he said, faintly remembering a long-ago message.

'The dramaturge who has a wonderful part for you,' she confirmed, 'if you have intelligence enough to accept it.' She patted his head in a friendly way, and stood up.

'If you want me for a part, you should talk to my agent,' he called after her.

'Oh, I did that, Rafiel. She threw me out.' Hillaree was rummaging through the heap of her discarded clothing on the bedside chair. She emerged with a lapcase, which she carried back to the bed. 'I admit this isn't going to be a *big* show,' she told him, squatting crosslegged on his bed as she opened the screen from the case. 'I'm not Mosay. I don't do spectacoli. But people are travelling out to the stars, Rafiel. The newest one is a habitat called *Hakluyt*. The whole population has voted to convert their habitat into an interstellar space vehicle—'

'I know about that!' he snapped, more or less truthfully. 'Habitat people have done that before — last year, wasn't it? Or a couple of years ago? I think one was going to Alpha Centauri or somewhere.'

'You see? You don't even remember. No one else does, either, and yet it's a grand, *heroic* story! These people are doing something hard and dangerous. No, Rafiel,' she finished, wagging her pretty head, 'it's the greatest story of

52

our time and it needs to be told *dramatically*, so people will *comprehend* it. And I'm the one to tell it, and you're the one to play it. Oh, it won't be like a Mosay production, I'll give you that. But you'll never again see anything as right for you as the part of the captain of the kosmojet *Hakluyt*.'

'I don't know anything about kosmojets, do I? Anyway, I can't. Mosay already had one cacafuega attack when he heard a rumour about it.'

'*Fichtig* Mosay. He and I don't do the same kind of thing. This one will be *intimate*, and *personal*. *Pas* music, *pas* dancing, *pas* songs. It will be a whole new departure for your career.'

'But a song-and-dance man is what I am!'

She sniffed at him. 'You're a short-timer, Rafiel. You're going to get *old*. Listen to me. This is where you need to go. I've watched you. I'm willing to bet my reputation—'

'Your reputation!'

She ignored the interruption. '—that you're just as good an actor as you are a dancer and singer . . . and, just to make you understand what's involved here, you can have five points on the gross receipts, which you know you'll *jamais* get from Mosay.'

'Five per cent of not very much is still very little,' Rafiel said at once, grinning at her to show that he meant no hard feelings.

She nodded as though she had expected that. She opened her bag and fingered the keypad for her screen. 'May I?' she said perfunctorily, not waiting for an answer. A scroll of legal papers began to roll up the screen. 'This is the deal for the first broadcast,' she said. 'That's twenty million dollars from right here on Earth, plus another twenty million for the first-run remotes. Syndication: that's a contract with a guarantee of another forty million over a ten-year period. And all that's a minimum, Rafiel; I'd bet anything that it'll double that. And there are the contracts for the sub rights – the merchandising, the music. Add it all up, and you'll see that the *guarantee* comes pretty close to a hundred million dollars. What's five per cent of that, Rafiel?'

The question was rhetorical. She wasn't waiting for an

53

answer. She was already scrolling to the next display, not giving Rafiel a chance to order her out of his condo. '*Là!*' she said. '*Voici!*'

What they were looking at on the screen was a habitat. It was not an impressive object to the casual view. As in all pictures from space, there was no good indication of size, and the thing might have been a beverage can, floating in orbit.

'There's where our story is,' she said. 'What you see there is habitat *Hakluyt*. It starts with a population of twenty thousand people, with room to expand to five times that. It's a whole small town, Rafiel. The kind of town they used to have in the old days before the arcologies, you know? A place with everybody knowing everybody else, interacting, loving, hating, dreaming – and totally cut off from everyone else. It's a microcosm of humanity, right there on *Hakluyt*, and we're going to tell its story.'

Although Rafiel was looking at the woman's pictures, he didn't think them very interesting. As far as Rafiel could tell, *Hakluyt* was a perfectly ordinary habitat, a stubby cylinder with the ribs for the pion tracks circling its outer shell. What he could tell wasn't actually very much. He hadn't spent much time on habitats, only one two-week visit, once, with – with . . . ? No, he had long since forgotten the name of the companion of that trip, and indeed everything about the trip itself except that habitats were not particularly luxurious places to spend one's time.

'How much spin does this thing have?' he asked, out of technical curiosity. 'I'm not used to dancing in light-G.'

'When it's en route *pas* spin at all. The gravity effect will be along the line of thrust. But you're forgetting, Rafiel,' she chided him. 'There won't be any dancing anyway. That's why this is such a breakthrough for you. This is a dramatic *story*, and you'll act it!'

'Hum,' said Rafiel, not pleased with this woman's continuing reminders that, in his special case, becoming older meant that it would become harder and harder for him to keep in dancer's kind of shape. 'Why do you say they're cut off from the rest of the world? Habitats are a lot easier to

54

get to than, *per esempio*, Mars. There's always a stream of ships going back and forth.'

'Not to this habitat,' Hillaree told him confidently. 'You're missing the point, and that's the whole drama of our story. You see that cluster of motors on the base? *Hakluyt* isn't just going to stay in orbit. *Hakluyt* will be going all the way to the star Tau Ceti. They'll be cut off, all right. They aren't coming back to the Earth, ever.'

As soon as the woman was out of his condo, unbedded but also unrejected, or at least not *finally* rejected in the way that most mattered to her, Rafiel was calling his agent to complain. Fruitlessly. It was a lot too early in the morning for Jeftha to be answering her tel. He tried again when he got to the rehearsal hall, with the same 'No Incoming' icon appearing on the screen. 'Bitch,' he said to the screen, though without any real resentment – Jeftha was as good a talent agent as he had ever had – and joined the rest of the cast.

They had started without him. Charlus was drilling the chorus all over again and Victorium, with Docilia standing by, was impatiently waiting for Rafiel himself. 'Now,' he said, 'if you're *quite* ready to go to work? Here's where we come to a tricky kind of place in *Oedipus*. You've ordered Creon banished, in spite of the fact that he's your brother-in-law. You think he lied to you about the prophecy from Apollo's priests, and you've just found out that your wife, Jocasta, is also your mother –'

'Victorium dear,' Docilia began, 'that's something I wanted to talk about. I don't have enough lines there, do I? Since it's *per certo* as big a shock to me too?'

'You'd have to talk to Mosay about that when he gets back, Docilia dear,' Victorium said. 'Can't we stick to the point? Besides the incest thing, Rafiel, you're the one who murdered her husband, who is also your real father –'

'I've read the script,' Rafiel told him.

'Of course you have, Rafiel dear,' Victorium said, sounding much less than confident of it. 'Then we follow you into Jocasta's room, and you see that she hung herself, out of shame.'

'Can't I do that on-screen, Vic?' Docilia asked. 'I mean, committing suicide's a really dramatic moment.'

'I don't think so, dear, but that's another thing you'd have to talk to Mosay about. Anyway, it's not the point right now, is it? I'm talking about what Rafiel does when he sees you've committed suicide.'

'I take the pins out of her hair and blind myself with them,' said Rafiel, nodding.

'Right. You jab the gold hairpins into your eyes. That's what I'm thinking about. What's the best way for us to handle that?'

'How do you mean?' Rafiel asked, blinking at him.

'Well, we want it to look *real*, don't we?'

'Sure,' Rafiel said, surprised, not understanding the point. That sort of thing was up to the computer synthesizers, which would produce any kind of effect anybody wanted.

Victorium was thoughtfully silent. Docilia cleared her throat. 'On second thought,' she said, 'maybe it's better if I hang myself offstage after all.'

Victorium stirred and gave her a serious look. Then he surrendered. 'We'll talk about all this stuff later,' he said. 'Let me get Charlus off everybody's back and we'll try putting the scene after that together.'

Rafiel was surprised to see Docilia give him a serious wink, but whatever she had on her mind had to wait. Victorium was calling them all together.

'All right,' he said, 'let's run it through. All the bad stuff is out in the open now. Rafiel knows what he's done, and all four of you kids are onstage now in the forgiveness scene. Ket, you're the Polyneices, take it from the top.'

Obediently the quartet formed and the boy began to sing:

POLYNEICES: We forgive you. If you doubt it, ask that zany Antigone, or Eteocles, or sweet Ismene.
ETEOCLES: You can't be all that bad.
ISMENE: After all, *vous êtes* our dad.

56

'Now you, Rafiel,' Victorium said, nodding, and Rafiel took up his lines.

OEDIPUS: Calm? *Come possibile* for me to be calm?
I've killed my pop and shtupped my dear old mom.
ANTIGONE: It's okay, dad, we're all with you.
It'll be a lousy life but we'll be true.
Wherever you go—

'No, no,' Charlus cried, breaking in. 'Excuse me, Victorium, but no. Bruta, this is *tap*, not ballet. Keep your feet down on the floor, will you?'

'*Aspet*'!' Victorium snapped. 'I'm running this rehearsal, and if you keep interrupting—'

'But she's ruining it, don't you see?' the choreographer pleaded. 'Just give me a minute with her. Please? Bruta, I want you to tap on the turn, and give us a little disco hip rotation when you sing. And I want to hear every tap all by itself, loud and clear. . . . '

There was, naturally, more objection from Victorium. Rafiel backed away to watch, not directly involved, and turned when he felt Docilia plucking at his arm.

'Be real careful,' she whispered. 'Don't let Mosay push you into anything. I think he wants you to really do it. The blinding,' she added impatiently when she saw that he hadn't understood.

Rafiel stared at her to see if she was joking. She wasn't. 'Believe me, that's what he wants from you,' she said, nodding. 'No faking it. He wants real blood. Real pain. Pieces of eyeball hanging out on your cheek.'

'Docilia!' he said, grimacing.

'*Was ist das* "Docilia"? *Voi sapete* how Mosay is. Oh, maybe he wouldn't expect you to *permanently* blind yourself. After the shooting was over he'd pay so the doctors could graft in some new eyes for you – but still.'

'Mosay wouldn't ask anybody to do that,' Rafiel protested.

'Wouldn't he? Especially considering— Well, when he comes back, just ask him,' she said, and stopped there.

Rafiel had grasped her meaning, anyway. Especially con-

57

sidering could only be that, in the long run, they were beginning to be looking on him as expendable.

When he finally did get through to his agent she was only perfunctorily apologetic. '*Mi scusi*,' Jeftha said. 'I had a hard night.' That was all the explanation she offered, but her dark and youthful face supported it. The skin was as unlined as always, but her eyes were red. 'Acrobats,' she said, wearily running one hand through her thick hedge of hair.

'You shouldn't sleep with your clients,' Rafiel said, setting aside the historical fact that she had, on occasion, with himself. 'Now, this woman Hillaree. . . . '

When Jeftha heard about the dramaturge's surprise visit she was furious. 'The *puta!*' she snapped. 'Going behind your agent's *back*? She'll never cast a client of mine again – but how could you, Rafiel? If Mosay finds out you've been dealing with a tuppenny tinhorn like Hillaree he'll go berserker!'

'I wasn't *dealing* with her,' Rafiel began, but she cut him off.

'Pray he doesn't hear about it. He's in a bad enough mood already. When he got to look at his locations somebody told him that the Thebes he was trying to match was the wrong Thebes – two of them with the same name, Rafiel, can you imagine that? How stupid can they be? The Thebes in Egypt didn't count. The Thebes somewhere north of Athens was the one where Oedipus had been king, and it was an entirely different kind of territory.'

'He's back?'

'He will be in the morning,' she confirmed. 'Now, was that what you were so *fou* to talk to me about?'

He hesitated, and then said, 'Forget it now, anyway.' Because he couldn't quite bring himself to ask her the question that was mostly on his mind, which was whether it was at all possible that Docilia's hints and implications could possibly be right.

58

8

The work of a dramaturge does not end with making sure a production is successfully performed. A major part of the job is making sure that audiences will want to spend their money to see it. In the furtherance of this endeavour, sweet are the uses of publicity; for which reason Mosay has arranged to do his first costumed rehearsals in a very conspicuous place. The place he has chosen is the public park on the roof of the arcology, where there are plenty of loungers and strollers, and every one a sure word-of-mouth broadcaster when they get home. Nor has Mosay failed to alert the paparazzi to be present in force.

Rafiel thought seriously of taking the kitten with him to show off at the day's rehearsal – after all, who else in the troupe owned a live cat? But the park was half a kilometre square, with a lake and a woodsy area and sweet little gardens all around. There was even a boxwood maze, great for children to play in, but all too good a place for a little kitten to get lost in, he decided, and regretfully left it in the care of his server.

The trouble with the rooftop was that it was windy. They were nearly a kilometre above the ground, where the air was always blowing strong. Clever vanes deflected the worst of the gusts, but not all of them; Rafiel felt chilled and wished Mosay had chosen another workplace. Or that, at least, they hadn't been instructed to show up in costume: there wasn't much warmth in the short woollen tunic. The winds were stronger than usual that day, and there were thick black clouds rolling toward them over the arcologies to the west. Rafiel listened: had he heard the sound of distant thunder? Or just the wind?

He shivered and joined the other performers as they walked around to get used to their costumes. Although the rooftop was the common property of all the hundred and sixty-odd thousand people who lived or worked in that particular arcology, Mosay had managed to persuade the arcology council to set one grassy sward aside for rehearsals. The council didn't object. They agreed that it would be a pleasing sort of entertainment for the tenants, and anyway Mosay was a first-rate persuader – after all, what other thing did a dramaturge really have to be?

The proof of his persuasive powers was that, astonishingly, everyone in the cast was there, and on time: Mosay himself, back from his fruitless quest but looking fresh and undaunted, and Victorium, and Charlus, the choreographer – no, *assistant* choreographer, Rafiel corrected himself resolutely – and all the eleven principal performers in the show and the dozen members of the chorus. Rafiel had practised with the sandals and the sword in his condo, while the watching kitten purred approvingly; by now he was easy enough in the costume. Not Andrev, the Creon, who kept getting his sword caught between his knees. There weren't any costume problems for Sander, the Tiresias, since his costume was only a long featureless smock, and Sander, who was a tall, unkempt man with seal-coloured hair that straggled down over his shoulders, wore the thing as though he were ignoring it, which was pretty much the way he wore all his clothes anyway. All the women wore simple white gowns, Docilia's Jocasta with flowers in her hair, the daughters unembellished.

But when Rafiel first saw Bruta, the Antigone, turn toward him his heart stopped for a moment, she was so like Alegretta. '*Che cosa*, Rafiel?' she asked in sudden worry at his expression, but he only shook his head. He kept watching her, though. Apart from the chance resemblance to his life's lost love, Bruta struck him as a bit of a puzzle. Bruta looked neither younger nor older than anyone else in the cast, of course – Rafiel himself always excepted – but it was obvious that she was a lot less experienced. That interested Rafiel. Mosay was not the kind who liked to bother with newcomers. He left the discovery of fresh talent to lesser dramaturges; he could afford to hire the best, who inevitably were also the ones who had long since made their

reputations. Rafiel thought of asking Docilia, who would be sure to know everyone's reasons for everything they did, but there wasn't time. Mosay was already waving everyone to cluster around him.

'Company,' said Mosay commandingly. 'I'm glad to be back, but we've got a lot of work to do, so if I may have your attention?' He got it and said sunnily, 'I do have one announcement before we begin. I've found our shooting location. *Wunderbar*, it has an existing set that we can use – oh, not *exactly* replicating old Thebes, in a technical sense, but close enough. And we'd better get on with it, so *if* you please. . . . ' Rafiel concealed a grin at the way Mosay was making sure he looked every centimetre the staging genius as he played to the spectators behind the velvet ropes, and, of course, to the pointing cameras of the paparazzi. When he had everyone's attention he went on. 'We aren't going to do the short fighting-the-Sphinx scene because we don't have a sphinx' – well, of course they didn't; there never would be a sphinx until the animation people put one in – 'so we'll start with the *pas de quatre*, where you kids' – nodding to the four 'children' of Oedipus and Jocasta – 'sing your little song about how after Oedipus saved Thebes from the Sphinx he married your *maman*, the widowed Jocasta, whose husband had been mysteriously murdered and thus Oedipus became *koenig* himself—'

'Oh, hell, Mosay,' said Docilia warmly, 'that's a whole play right there. *Bisogniamo* say all that?'

'We must. We'll get it in, and anyway that's not your problem, Docilia, is it? In fact, you're not even in this scene, or the next scene either, except to stand around and look pretty, because this is where Creon makes his entrance and tells Oedipus what the oracle of Apollo said.'

'I already know all the Creon lines,' Andrev said proudly. He had the reputation of being a slow study.

'I certainly hope so, Andrev. Places, everybody? And now if we'll just take it from the last bars of Victorium's opening. . . . '

It wasn't a big scene for Rafiel. He didn't even get to make a real entrance, just ambled onstage to wait for Creon to show up. The scene belonged to the Creon. Victorium had written the music accordingly, with a background score full of dark and mystical dissonances – right enough for an oracle's pronouncements, Rafiel supposed.

What Creon brought was bad news, so Rafiel's responses had to be equally sombre. Not just sombre, though. Rafiel made sure all his gestures were, well, a trifle less *portentous* than the Creon's – after all, Rafiel was not merely playing an old, doomed Theban king, he was playing *himself* playing the king. That was what being a star was all about.

Rafiel flinched at a boom from the sky. Thunder was crashing somewhere in the distance, and Mosay agitatedly demanded of a watching arcology worker that they erect the dome. Just in time; rain was slashing down on the big transparent hood over the roof before the petalled sections had quite closed over them. Rafiel shuddered again. He found that he was feeling quite tired. He wondered if it was showing up in his performance . . . though of course it was only a dress rehearsal.

All the same, Rafiel didn't like the feeling that his dancing was not as lively – as bumptiously clumsy – as his audiences expected of him. He forced himself into the emotions of the part – easily enough, because Rafiel had all the ambiguity of any actor in his beliefs. Whatever he privately thought or felt, he could throw himself into the thoughts and feelings of the character he was playing; and if that character took silly oracular conundrums seriously, then for the duration of that role so would Rafiel. He worked so hard at it that at the end of the third run-through he was sweating as he finished his meditative *pas de seul*. So was the Creon, although he had no dancing to do. But it was Rafiel Mosay was watching, with a peculiar expression of concern on his face, and it was Rafiel he was looking at when he declared a twenty-minute break.

'*Comment ça va?*' Docilia asked, taking Rafiel's elbow.

He blinked at her. 'Fine, fine,' he assured her, though he didn't think he really was. Was it that obvious? He hadn't missed Mosay's watchful eyes, though now the dramaturge had forgotten him in the press of making quick calls on the communications monitor at the edge of the meadow. Rafiel made an effort and pressed Docilia's arm against his side amatively – well, maybe there was his problem right there, he thought. Deprivation. After all, why should any healthy person deliberately stop having sex, thus very possibly endangering not only his performance but even his health?

'You don't *look* all right,' Docilia told him, steering him through the park to a formal garden. 'Except when you're looking at that Bruta.'

'Oh, now really,' Rafiel laughed – actually laughing, because the thought really amused him. 'She's just so *young*.'

'So amateurish, you mean.'

'That too,' he acknowledged, slipping his arm around her waist in a friendly way. 'I'm surprised Mosay took her on.'

'You don't know?'

'Know what?' Rafiel asked, proving that he did not.

'She's his latest daughter,' Docilia informed him with pleasure. 'So if you're shtupping her you're going to be part of the family.'

Rafiel opened his mouth to deny that he was making love to Bruta, or indeed to anyone else since the last time with Docilia herself, but he closed it again. That, after all, was none of Docilia's business, not to mention that it did not comport well with the image of a lusty, healthy, *youthful* idol of every audience.

But she might have been reading his own. 'Oh, poor Rafiel,' she said, tightening her grip on his waist. 'You're just not getting enough, are you?' She looked around. There was hardly anyone near them, the casual spectators mostly still watching the performers in the rehearsal area. And they were near the maze.

'I have an idea,' she murmured. 'Can we go in the maze for a while?'

After all, why not? Rafiel surrendered. 'I'd like nothing better,' he said gallantly, knowing as well as she did that the best thing one did in the isolation of a maze was to do a little friendly fooling around with one's companion – on whom, in any case, Rafiel was beginning to feel he might as well be beginning to have sexual designs again, after all. They had no trouble finding a quiet dead end and, without discussion, Rafiel unhesitatingly put his hand on her.

'Are you sure you aren't too tired?' she asked, but turning toward him as she spoke; and, of course, that imposed on him the duty to prove that he wasn't tired at all. He realized he didn't have much time to demonstrate it in, so they wasted none. They were horizontal on the warm, grassy ground in a minute.

It was strange, he reflected, pumping away, that something you wanted to do could also be a wearisome chore. He was glad enough when they had finished. . . . And almost at that very moment, as though taking a quick cue, a voice from an unseen person, somewhere else in the maze, was thundering at them.

It was Mosay's voice. What he was saying – bawling – was: 'Rafiel! Is that you I hear in there with Docilia? Come out this minute! We need to talk.'

Rafiel was breathing hard, but he managed to grin at his partner and help her to her feet. 'Can't it wait, Mosay?' he called, carefully conserving his breath.

'It can *not*,' the dramaturge roared. '*Expliquez* yourself. Who's this woman who's claiming she's got you signed up for a new production?'

Rafiel groaned. Mosay had in fact found out. Docilia put an alarmed hand on his forearm.

'Oh, *paura*. You'd better pull yourself together,' she whispered, doing the same for herself. 'He's really *furioso* about something.'

Rafiel gave in, tugging his underpants back on. 'Well,' he called to the featureless hedge, 'we did talk a little bit, she and I—'

'She says you *agreed*!' snapped the invisible Mosay. 'She's got a story about it in all the media, and I won't have it! Rafiel, you're making me look like a *dummkopf.*'

'I never actually agreed—'

'But you didn't say no, either, did you? That's not *cosi*

65

buono. I won't have you making *any* commitments after this one,' Mosay roared. 'Now *vieni qui* and talk to me!'

His muttering died in the distance. Docilia turned to look into Rafiel's face. 'What in the world have you done?' she asked.

'Nothing,' he said positively, and then, thinking it over, 'But I guess enough.' He could have thrown the woman out of his home without any discussion at all, he thought. He hadn't. Resigned, he braced himself for the vituperation that was sure to come.

It came, all right, but not as pure vituperation. Mosay had switched to another mode. 'Oh, *pauvre petit* Rafiel,' he said sorrowfully, 'haven't I always done everything I can for you? And now you're conspiring behind my back with some sleazeball for a cheap-and-dirty exploitation show?'

'It isn't really that cheap, Mosay, it's a hundred mil—'

'Cheap isn't just *money*, Rafiel. Cheap is cheap *people*. Second-raters. Do you want to wind up your career with the has-beens and never-wases? No, Rafiel,' he said, shaking his head, '*Non credo* you want that. And, anyway, I've talked to your agent, and Jeftha says the deal's already *kaput*.' He allowed himself a forgiving smile, then turned away briskly.

'Now let's get some work done here, company,' he called, clapping his hands. 'One more time, from Creon's story about the oracle....'

But they didn't actually get that far, and it was Rafiel's fault.

Rafiel started out well enough, rising in wrath to sing his attack on Creon's message from the oracle. Then something funny happened. Rafiel felt the ground sliding away underneath him. He didn't feel the impact of his head on the grassy lawn. He didn't know he had lost consciousness. He was only aware of beginning to come to, half dazed, as someone was – someones were – loading him on to a high-wheeled cart and hurrying him to an elevator, and walking beside him were people who were agitatedly talking about him as though he couldn't hear.

'You'll have to tell him, Mosay,' said Docilia's voice, fuzzily registering in Rafiel's ears.

66

Then there was a mumble, of which all Rafiel could distinguish was when, at the end, someone raised his voice to say, '*Pas* me!'

'*Allora* who?' in Docilia's voice again, and a longer mumble mumble, and then once more Docilia: 'I think it'd be better from *la donna.* . . . '

And then he felt the quick chill spray of an anaesthetic on the side of his neck. Rafiel fell asleep as the shot did its job. Deeply asleep. So deep that there was no need to worry about anything . . . and no desire to wonder just what it was that his friends had been talking about.

'Just fatigue,' the doctor said reassuringly when Rafiel was conscious again. 'You collapsed. *Probabilmente* you've just been working too hard.'

'Probably?' Rafiel asked, challenging the woman, but she only shrugged.

'You're just as good as you were when you left here, basically,' she said. 'Your *ami*'s here to take you home.'

The *ami* was Mosay, full of concern and sweetness. Rafiel was glad to see him.

'I'm sorry about being so silly, but I'll be ready to get back to work in the morning,' Rafiel promised, leaning on the hard, strong form of the nurser.

'*Sans doute* you will,' Mosay said worriedly. 'Here, sit in the *chaise*, let the nurser give you a ride to the cars.' And at the elevator, taking over the wheelchair himself: 'Still,' he added, 'if you're at all tired, why shouldn't you take another day or two to rest? I've picked a location spot in Texas. . . . '

That roused Rafiel. 'Texas? *Pas* Turkey?'

'Of course not Turkey,' Mosay said severely. 'There's just the right place out in the desert, hardly built up at all. Now, here we are at your place, and they've got your nice bed all ready for you – *gesu cristo*!' he interrupted himself, staring. 'What's that?'

Weak as he was, Rafiel laughed out loud. His server was coming toward him welcomingly, and padding regally after, tail stiff in the air, was the kitten.

67

'It's just my cat, Mosay. A present from a friend.'

'Does it bite?' When reassured, the dramaturge gave it a hostile look anyway, as though suspecting an attack or, worse, an excretion. 'If that's what you like, Rafiel, why should I criticize? Anyway, I'll leave you now. You can join us when you're ready. We'll work around you for a bit. No, don't argue, it's no trouble. Just give me your word that you won't come out until you're *absolutely* ready. . . . '

'I promise,' said Rafiel, wondering why it felt so good to be undertaking to do nothing for a while. It never had before.

9

*Rafiel, who loves to travel, seldom has time to do much of it.
That seems a bit strange, since he is a famous presence in all the
places where human beings live, on planet and off, but of course
his presence in almost all of those places is only electronic. He is
looking forward eagerly to the ride in the magnetrain, with no
one for company but the little white kitten. When he finally
embarks, after the obligate few days of loafing around his condo,
it really is as great a pleasure for him as he had hoped — well,
would have been, anyway, if he weren't continuing to be so
unreasonably tired. Still, he enjoys watching the scenery flash by
at six hundred kilometres an hour — arcologies, fields, woods,
rivers — and he enjoys doing nothing. He especially enjoys being
alone. With his presence on the train unknown to the fans who
might otherwise besiege him, with only the servers to bring his
meals and make up his bed and tend to the kitten, he thinks he
almost would not mind if the trip went on for ever. When they
reach their destination at the edge of the Sonora Desert he is
reluctant to get off.*

Rafiel arrived at the Sonora arcology just in time to catch
a few hour's sleep in a rented condo, not nearly as nice as
his own, in an arcology an order of magnitude tinier. When
he reported for work in the morning even Turkey began to
seem more desirable. This desert was *hot*.

Mosay was there to greet him solicitously — proudly, too,
as he waved around the set he had discovered. '*Wunderbar*,
isn't it? And such *bonne chance* it was available. Of course,
it's not an *exact* copy of the actual old Thebes, but I think
it's quite *interessante*, don't you? And there's no sense casting
great talents, is there, if you're going to ask them to play in
front of a background of dried mud huts.'

Wilting in the heat, Rafiel gazed around at Mosay's idea
of an 'interesting' Thebes. He was pretty sure that Thebes-

in-Sonora didn't much resemble the old Thebes-in-Boe-otia. So much marble! So much artfully concealed lighting inside the buildings – did the Greeks have artificial lighting at all? Would the Greeks have put that heroic-seized statue of Oedipus (actually, of Rafiel himself in his Oedipus suit) in the central courtyard? And, if they had, would they have surrounded it with banked white and yellow roses? Did they have *moats* around their castles? Well, did they have castles at all? Questions like that took Rafiel's mind off the merci-less sun, but not enough.

'It's you and Docilia now, please,' Mosay said – com-manded, really. 'Places!' And on cue Docilia began Jocasta's complaint about childbirth. Rafiel reacted as the part called for as, shoulders swaying, head accusingly erect, she sang:

> *Che sapete*, husband? I did all the borning,
> Carrying those devils and puking every morning.
> Never *peine* so *dur*, never agony so hot,
> It was like pushing a pumpkin through—

'No, no, cut,' Mosay shouted. 'Oh, Rafiel! What do you think you're doing there, taking a little nap? Your wife's giving you hell about the kids she's borne for you and you're gaping around like some kind of *turista*. Get a little movement into it, will you?'

'Sorry,' Rafiel said, as the cast relaxed. He saw Charlus coming, deferentially but with determination, toward him, as he turned his face to the server that came over to mop the sweat off his brow. There wasn't much of it, in spite of the heat; in the dry desert air it evaporated almost as fast as it formed.

'Do you mind, Rafiel?' Charlus offered, almost begging. 'I was just thinking, you might want to wring your turn out and let the arms go all the way through when she starts the "puking every morning" line.'

'I didn't want to upstage her.'

'No, of course not, but Mosay's got this idea that you have to be *interacting*, you see, and—'

'Sure,' Rafiel said. 'Let's get on with it.' And he was able

71

to keep his mind on his work, in spite of the heat, in spite of the fatigue, for nearly another hour. But by the time Mosay called a break for lunch he was feeling dizzy.

Instantly the sexy young Bruta was at his side. 'Let me keep you company,' she said, almost purring as she guided him to a seat in the shade. 'What would you like? I'll bring you a plate.'

'I'm not really hungry,' he said, with utter truth. He didn't think he would ever be hungry again.

Bruta was all sympathy. 'No, of course not. It is dreadfully hot, isn't it? But maybe just a plate of ice cream – do you like palmfruit?' He gave in, and watched her go for it with objective admiration. The girl was slim as an eel, with a tiny bum that any man would enjoy getting his hands on. But it was only objectively that the thought was interesting; nothing stirred in his groin, no pictures of an interesting figure developed in the crystal ball of his mind. Only—

His mouth was filling with thin, warm saliva.

It could not be possible that he was about to vomit, he thought, and then realized it was quite possible, in fact. He got briskly to his feet, prepared to give a closed-lipped smile to anyone who was looking at him. No one was. He turned away from the direction of the buffet table, heading out into the desert. As he got behind Oedipus's castle he picked up his pace, pressing the palm of his hand against his involuntarily opening mouth, but he couldn't hold it. He bent forward and spewed a cupful of thin, colourless fluid on to the thirsty sand.

It wasn't painful to vomit. It was almost a pleasure, it happened so easily and quickly, and when it was over he felt quite a lot better – though puzzled, for he hadn't eaten enough that morning to have enough in his stomach to be worth vomiting.

He turned to see if any of the troupe had been looking in his direction. Apparently no human had, but a server was hurrying toward him across the desert. 'Sir?' Its voice was humble but determined. 'Sir, do you need assistance here?'

'No. *Hsieh-hsieh*,' Rafiel added, remembering to be courteous as ever, even to machines.

'I must tell you that there is some risk to your safety here,' the server informed him. 'We have destroyed or removed fourteen small reptiles and other animals this morning, but others may come in. They are attracted by the presence of warm-blooded people. Please be careful where you step.'

Rafiel almost forgot his distress, charmed by the interesting idea. 'You mean "rattlesnakes"? I've heard of rattlesnakes. They can bite a person and kill him.'

'Oh, hardly kill one, sir, since we are equipped for quick medical attention. But it would be a painful experience, so if you don't mind rejoining the others . . . ?'

And it paced him watchfully, all the way back.

It didn't seem that anyone had noticed, though Bruta was standing there with a tray in her hand. 'Nothing to eat after all, please,' Rafiel begged her. 'It's just too hot.'

'Whatever you say, Rafiel,' she said submissively. But she stayed attentively by him all through the break, watchful as any serving machine. And when they started again he saw the girl reporting to her father, and felt Mosay's eyes studying him.

He managed to keep his mind on what he was doing for that shot, and for the next. It was, he thought, a creditable enough performance, but it wasn't easy. They were shooting out of sequence, to take advantage of the lighting as the sun moved and for grouping the actors conveniently. Rafiel found that confusing. Worse, he discovered that he was feeling strangely detached. Docilia did not seem to be the Docilia he had so often bedded any more. She had become her role: Jocasta, the mother of his children and appallingly also of himself. When he reached the scene where he confronted her dead body, twisting as it hung in the throneroom, he felt an unconquerable need for reassurance. Without thinking, he reached out and touched her to make sure she was still warm.

'Oh, *merde*, Rafiel,' she sighed, opening her eyes to stare at him, 'what are you doing? You've wrecked the whole *drecklich* shot.'

But Mosay was there already, soothing, a little apprehensive. 'It's all right, Rafiel,' he said. 'I know this is hard on you, the first day's shooting, and all this heat. It's about time to quit for the day, anyway.'

Rafiel nodded. 'It'll be better in the morning,' he promised.

But it wasn't.

It wasn't better the next day, or the day after that, or the day after that one. It didn't get better at all. 'It's the heat, of course,' Docilia told him, watching Charlus trying to perfect the chorus in their last appearance ('Deeper *plié*, for God's sake – *use* your legs!'). 'Imagine Mosay making us work in the *open*, for God's sake.'

'Of course,' Rafiel agreed. He had stopped trying to look as though he were all right when he was off camera. He just stood in the shade, with an air cooler blowing on him. And Charlus said the same thing.

'You'll be all right when we finish here,' he promised, watching Bruta and the Ismene. 'It's only another day or two – no, no! *Chassé* back now! Then a *pas de chat*, but throw your legs back and come down on the right foot – that's better. Don't you want to lie down, Rafiel?'

He did want that, of course. He wanted it a lot, but not enough to be seen doing it on the set. He did all his lying down when shooting was over for the day, back in the borrowed condo, where he slept almost all the free time he had, with the kitten curled up at his feet.

Even Docilia was mothering him, coming to tuck him in at night but making it clear that she was not intending, or even willing, to stay. She kissed him on the forehead and hesitated, looking at the purring kitten. 'You got that from Alegretta, didn't you? *Permesso* ask you something?' And when he nodded, 'No offence, Rafiel, but why are you so *verrückt* for this particular one?'

'You mean Alegretta? I don't know,' he said, after thought. '*Forse* it's just because she's so different from us. She doesn't even talk like us. She's – serious.'

'Oh, Rafiel? Aren't we serious? We work *hard*.'

'Well, sure we do, but it's just – well – you know, we're just sort of making shadow pictures on a screen. Maybe it

comes to what she's serious *about*,' he offered. 'You know, she started a whole new life for herself – quit medicine, took up science. . . . '

Docilia sniffed. 'That's not so unusual. I could do that if I wanted to. Some day I probably will.'

Rafiel smiled up at her, imagining this pale, tiny beauty becoming a scientist. 'When?' he asked.

'What does it matter when? I've got plenty of time!'

And Rafiel fell asleep thinking about what 'plenty of time' meant. It meant, among other things, that when you had for ever to get around to *important* things, it gave you a good reason to postpone them – for ever.

The shooting went faster than Rafiel had imagined, and suddenly they were at an end to it. As he waited in full make-up for his last scene, his face a ruin, himself unable to see through the wreck the make-up people had made of his eyes, Docilia came over. 'You've been wonderful,' she told him lovingly. 'I'm glad it's over, though. I promise you I won't be sorry to leave here.'

Rafiel nodded and said, more wistfully than not, 'Still it's kind of nice to have a little solitude sometimes.'

She gave him a perplexed look. 'Solitude,' she said, as though she'd never heard the word before.

Then Mosay was calling for him on the set . . . and then, before he had expected it, his part was done. Old Oedipus, blinded and helpless, was cast out of the city where he had reigned, and all that was left for the cast to shoot was the little come-on Mosay had prepared for the audiences, when the children and chorus got together to set up the sequel.

They didn't need Rafiel for that, but he lingered to watch, sweltering or not. A part of him was glad the ordeal was over. Another part was sombrely wondering what would happen next in his life. Back to the hospital for more tinkering, most likely, he thought, but there was no pleasure in that. He decided not to think about it and watched the shooting of the final scene. One after another the minor actors were telling the audience they hoped they'd liked the show, and then, all together:

76

If so, we'll sure do more of these
Jazzy old soaps by Mr Sophocles.

And that was it. They left the servers to strike the set.
They got on the blessedly cool cast bus that took them back
to the condo. Everyone was chattering, getting ready for the
farewells. And Mosay came stumbling down the aisle to
Rafiel, holding on to the seats. He leaned over, looking at
Rafiel carefully. 'Docilia says you wanted to stay here for a
bit,' he said.

That made Rafiel blink. What had she told him that for?
'Well, I only said I kind of liked being alone here. . . . '

The dramaturge was shaking his head masterfully. 'No,
no. It's quite all right, there's nothing left but the technical
stuff. I insist. You stay here. Rest. Take a few days here. I
think you'll agree it's worth it, and – and – anyway, *ese*,
after all, there's no real reason why you have to go back
with us, is there?'

And, on thinking it over, Rafiel realized that there actually
wasn't.

The trouble was that there wasn't any real reason to stay
in the Sonora arcology, either. As far as Rafiel could see,
there wasn't any reason for him to be anywhere at all,
because – for the first time in how long? – he didn't have
anything he had to do.

Since he'd had no practice at doing nothing, he made up
things to do. He called people on the tel screen. Called old
acquaintances – all of them proving to be kind, and solicitous, and quite unprecedentedly remote – called colleagues,
even called a few paparazzi, though only to thank them for
things they had already publicized for him and smilingly
secretive about any future plans.

Future plans reminded him to call his agent. Jeftha, at
least, seemed to feel no particular need to be kind. 'I had
the idea you were pretty sick,' she said, studying him with
care, and no more than half accepting his protestations that
he was actually entirely well and ready for more work quite
soon.

She shook her head at that. 'I've called off all your appearances,' she said. 'Let them get hungry, then when you're ready to get back—'

'I'm ready now!'

The black and usually cheerful face froze. 'No,' she said.

It was the first time his agent had ever said a flat 'no' to her best client. 'Ay Jesus,' he said, getting angry, 'who the hell do you think you're talking to? I don't need *you*.'

The expression on Jeftha's face became contrite. 'I know you don't, *caro mio*, but I need you. I need you to be well. I – care about you, dear Rafiel.'

That stopped the flooding anger in its tracks. He studied her suspiciously but, almost for the first time, she seemed to be entirely sincere. It was not a quality he had associated with agents.

'Anyway,' she went on, the tone becoming more the one he was used to, 'I can't let you make deals by yourself, *piccina*. You'll get involved with people like that stupid Hillaree and her dumb story ideas. Who wants to hear about *real* things like kosmojets going off to other stars? People don't care about *now*. They want the good old stories with lots of pain and torture and *dying* – excuse me, *carissimo*,' she finished, flushing.

But she was right. Rafiel thought that he really ought to think about that: was that the true function of art, to provide suffering for people who were incapable of having any?

He probably would think seriously about that, he decided, but not just yet. So he did very little. He made his calls, and between calls he dozed, and loafed, and pulled a string across the carpeted floor to amuse the kitten, and now and then remembered to eat.

He began to think about an almost forgotten word that kept popping up in his mind. The word was 'retirement'.

It was a strange concept. He had never known anyone who had 'retired'. Still, he knew that people used to do it in the old days. It might be an interesting novelty. There was no practical obstacle in the way; he had long since accumulated all the money he could possibly need to last him out . . . for whatever time he had left to live. (After all, it wasn't as though he were going to live for ever). Immortals had to worry about eternities, yes, but the cold fact was that no untreated human lasted much more than a hundred and twenty years, and Rafiel had already used up ninety of them.

He could even, he mused, be *like* an immortal in these declining years of his life. Just like an immortal, he could, if he liked, make a midcourse change. He could take up a new career and thus change what remained of his life entirely. He could be a writer, maybe; he was quite confident that any decent performer could do *that*. Or he could be a politician. Certainly enough people knew the name of the famous Rafiel to give him an edge over almost any other candidate for almost any office. In short, there was absolutely nothing to prevent him from trying something completely different with the rest of his life. He might fail at whatever he tried, of course. But what difference did that make, when he would be dead in a couple of decades anyway?

When the doorwarden rang he was annoyed at the interruption, since his train of thought had been getting interesting. He lifted his head in anger to the machine. '*Ho detto* positively, no calls!'

The doorwarden was unperturbed. 'There is always an exception,' it informed him, right out of its basic programming, 'in the case of visitors with special urgency, and I am informed this is one. The woman says she is from *Hakluyt* and she states that she is certain you will wish to see her.'

'*Hakluyt?* Is it that *fou* dramaturge woman again? Well, she's wrong about that, I don't want to talk about her stupid show—'

But then the voice from the speaker changed. It wasn't the doorwarden's any more. It was a human voice, and a familiar, female human voice at that. 'Rafiel,' she said fondly, 'what is this crap about a show? It's me, Alegretta. I came to visit you all the way from my ship *Hakluyt*, and I don't know anything about any stupid shows. Won't you please tell your doorwarden to let me in?'

10

Rafiel knows that Alegretta has come from somewhere near Mars, and he knows pretty well how far away Mars is from the Earth: many millions of kilometres. He knows how long even a steady-thrust spacecraft takes to cross that immense void between planets, and then how long it takes for a passenger to descend to a spaceport and get to this remote outpost on the edge of the Sonoran desert. And he is well able to count back the days and see that Alegretta must have started this trip to his side – at the very least – ten days or two weeks before, which is to say right around the time when he collapsed into the hospital back in Indiana. He knows all that, and understands its unpleasing implications. He just doesn't want to think about any of those implications at that moment.

When you have lost the love of your life and suddenly, without warning, she appears in it again, what do you do?

First, of course, there is kissing, and *It's been so long*s, and *How good it is to see you*s, and of course Alegretta has to see how well the kitten she sent is doing, and Rafiel has to admire the fat white cat Alegretta has brought with her, a server carrying it for her in a great screened box (it has turned out to be the kitten's mother), and of course Rafiel has to offer food and drink, and Alegretta has to accept something . . . but then what? What – after half a century or more – do you *say* to each other? What Rafiel said, watching his love nibble on biscuits and monkey-orange and beer, was only, 'I didn't expect you here.'

'Well, I had to come,' she said, diffident, smiling, stroking the snow-white cat that lay like a puddle in her lap, 'because Nicolette here kept rubbing up against me to tell me that she really missed her baby kitten – and because, oh, Rafiel, I've been so damn much missing *you*.' Which of course led to more kissing over the table, and while the server was cleaning up the beer that had got spilled in the process, Rafiel sank back to study her. She hadn't changed. The hair was a darker red now, but it was still Alegretta's unruly curly-mop hair, and the face and the body that went with the hair were not one hour older than they had been – sixty? seventy? however many years it had been since they last touched like this. Rafiel felt his heart trembling in his chest and said quickly, 'What were you saying about *Hakluyt*?'

'My ship. Yes.'

'You're going on that *ship*?'

'Of course I am, dear.' And it turned out that she was, though such a thing had never occurred to him when he was talking to the dramaturge woman. There definitely was a *Hakluyt* habitat, and it really was, even now, being fitted with lukewarm-fusion drives and a whole congeries of pion generators that were there to produce the muons that would make the fusion reactor react.

'You know all this nuclear fusion stuff?' Rafiel asked, marvelling.

'Certainly I do. I'm the head engineer on the ship, Rafiel,' she said with pride, 'and I'm afraid that means I can't stay here long. They're installing the drive engines right now, and I must be there before they finish.'

He shook his head. 'So now you've become a particle physicist.'

'Well, an engineer, anyway. Why not? You get tired of one thing, after you've done it for ninety or a hundred years. I just didn't want to be a doctor any more; when things go right it's boring, and when they don't—'

She stopped, biting her lip, as though there were something she wanted to say. Rafiel headed her off. 'But what will you find when you get to this distant what's-its-name star?'

'It's called Tau Ceti.'

'This Tau Ceti. What do you expect? Will people be able to live there?'

She thought about that. 'Well, yes, certainly they will – in the habitat, if nothing else. The habitat doesn't care what star it orbits. We do know there are planets there, too. We don't know, really, if any of them has life. . . . '

'But you're going anyway?'

'What else is there to do?' she asked, and he laughed.

'You haven't changed a bit,' he said fondly.

'Of course not. Why should I?' She sounded almost angry – perhaps at Rafiel because, after all, he had. He shook his head, reached for her with loving hunger, and pulled her to him.

Of course they made love, with the cat and the kitten watching interestedly from the chaise longue at the side of the room. Then they slept a while, or Alegretta did, because she was still tired from the long trip. Remarkably, Rafiel was not in the least tired. He watched over her tenderly, allowing himself to be happy in spite of the fact that he knew why she was there.

She didn't sleep long, and woke smiling up at him. 'I'm sorry, Rafiel,' she said.

'What have you got to be sorry for?'

'I'm sorry I stayed away so long. I was afraid, you see.' She sat up, naked. 'I didn't know if I could handle seeing you, well, grow old.'

Rafiel felt embarrassment. 'It isn't pretty, I suppose.'

'It's frightening,' she said honestly. 'I think you're the main reason I gave up medicine.'

'It's all right,' he said, soothing. 'Anyway, I'm sure what you're doing now is more interesting. Going to another *star*! It takes a lot of courage, that.'

'It takes a lot of hard work.' Then she admitted, 'It takes courage, too. It certainly took me a long time to make up my mind to do it. Sometimes I still wonder if I have the nerve to go through with it. We'll be thirty-five years en route, Rafiel. Nearly five thousand people, all packed together for that long.'

He frowned. 'I thought somebody said the *Hakluyt* was supposed to have twenty thousand to start.'

'We were. We are. But there aren't that many volunteers for the trip, you see. That's why they made me chief engineer; the other experts didn't see any reason to leave the solar system, when they were doing so many interesting things here.' She leaned forward to kiss him. 'Do you know what my work is, Rafiel? Do you know anything about lukewarm-fusion?'

'Well,' he began, and then honestly finished: 'No.'

She looked astonished, or perhaps it was just pitying. 'But there are powerplants in every arcology. Haven't you ever visited one?' She didn't wait for an answer but began to tell him about her work, and how long she had had to study to master the engineering details. And in his turn he told her about his life as a star, with the personal appearances and the fans always showing up, wherever he went, with their love and excitement; and about the production of *Oedipus* they had just finished, and the members of the troupe. Alegretta was fascinated by the inside glimpses of the lives of the famous. Then, when he got to the point of telling her about Docilia and her decision to try monogamy with the father of her child, as soon as the child was born, anyway, Alegretta began to purse her lips again. She got up to stare out the window.

He called, 'Is something wrong?'

She was silent for a moment, then turned to him seriously. 'Rafiel, dear,' she said. 'There's something I have to tell you.'

'I know,' he said reluctantly.

'No, I don't think you do. I didn't come here by accident. Mosay—'

He was beside her by then, and closed her lips with a kiss. 'But I do know,' he said. 'Mosay called you to tell you, didn't he? Why else would you come all the way back to Earth in such a great hurry? That little episode I had, it wasn't just fatigue, was it? It meant they can't keep me going much longer, so the bad news is that I don't have much time left, do I? I'm going to die.'

'Oh, Rafiel,' she said, woebegone.

'But I've known that this was going to happen all my life,' he said reasonably, 'or at least since you told me. It's all right.'

'It *isn't!*'

He shrugged, almost annoyed. 'It has to be all right, because I'm mortal,' he explained.

She was shaking her head. 'Yes. But no.' She seemed almost near tears as she plunged on. 'Don't you see, that's why I came here like this. You don't have to die *completely*. There's a kind of immortality that even short-timers have open to them if they want it. Like your Docilia.'

He frowned at her, and she reached out and touched his lips. 'Will you give me a baby?' she whispered. 'A son? A boy who will look just like you when he grows up – around Tau Ceti?'

11

Although the Sonora arcology is far tinier and dingier than some of those in the busy, crowded north, it naturally does not lack any of the standard facilities – including a clinic for implanting a human foetus into a nurturing animal womb. On the fourth day after the donation the new parents (or, usually, at least one of them) may come up to the sunny, brightly painted nursery to receive their foetus. It is true that the circumstances for Rafiel and Alegretta are a bit unusual. Most foetuses are implanted at once into the large mammal – a cow most often, or a large sow – that will bring them to term and deliver them. Their child has a more complicated incubation in store. He (it is definitely to be a boy, and they have spent a lot ot time thinking of names for him) must go with Alegretta to the interstellar ship Hakluyt, *which means that the baby's host must go there too. Cows are not really very portable. So, just for now, for the sake of ease in transportation, their foetus has been temporarily implanted in a much smaller mammal, which is now spending as much time as it is allowed sitting purring in Alegretta's lap, a bit ruffled at recent indignities, but quite content.*

They didn't just talk and make love and babies. On the second day Alegretta announced she was temporarily going to be a doctor again.

'But you've probably forgotten how to do it,' Rafiel said, half joking.

'The computer hasn't,' she told him, not joking at all. She got his medical records from the datafile and studied them seriously for a long time. Then she sent the server out for some odds and ends. When they came she pressed sticky sensor buttons on his chest and belly – 'I hope I remember how to do this without pulling all your hair off,' she said – and pored over the readings on her screen. Then she had long conversations over the tel with someone, from which Rafiel was excluded and which wound up in the server bringing him new little bottles of spansules and syrups to take. 'These will make you feel better,' she told him.

But they both knew that even the best efforts of loving Alegretta could not possibly make him *be* better.

They were also both well aware that they could not stay long together in Sonora. If they hadn't known that, they would have been told so, because the callback lists kept piling up on the communications screen – Mosay and Jeftha and ten or twelve others for Rafiel, faxed messages from *Hakluyt* for Alegretta. Once a day they took time to read them, and occasionally to answer them. 'They're putting the frozen stocks on board now,' Alegretta announced to her lover, between callbacks.

'Frozen food for the trip? You must need a lot—'

'No, no. Not food – well, a little bit of frozen food, yes, but we couldn't carry enough to last out the trip. Most of the food we need we'll grow along the way. What I'm talking about is frozen sperm and ova – cats, dogs, livestock, birds – and frozen seeds and clones for planting. We'll need them when we get there.'

'And what if there's no good planet there to plant them on?' he asked.

'Bite your tongue,' she said absently, making him smile at her as she sat huddled over the manifest. He found himself smiling a good deal these days. His kitten, which had not let either of them out of its sight while its mother was off in the implantation clinic, was licking its left forepaw with concentrated attention. The lovers touched a lot, sometimes talking, sometimes just drowsing in the scents and warmths of each other. They looked at each other a lot, charmed to see in each other a prospective parent of a shared child.

Rafiel said meditatively, 'It would have been fun to conceive it in the old-fashioned way.'

She looked up. 'It's safer when they do it in the laboratory. Not to mention this way we can be sure it's a boy.'

She came over and kissed him. 'Anyway, we can – well, in a day or two we can – do all of that we want to.'

Rafiel rubbed his ear against her cheek, quite content. It was a very minor inconvenience that sexual intercourse had to be postponed a bit, Alegretta's womb tender from the removal of the ovum.

'Are you getting restless?' she asked.

'Me? No, I'm happy to stay right here in the condo. Are you?'

She said, 'Not really, but there is something I'd like to do outside.'

'Name it.'

'It's so you'll know what my work's like,' she explained. 'If you think you'd like to, I'd enjoy showing you what this arcology's powerplant looks like.'

'Of course,' he said.

He would have said the same to almost anything Alegretta proposed. Still, it wasn't the kind of 'of course' he felt totally confident about, because one of Mosay's calls had been to warn him that the paparazzi knew he was still in the arcology. They somehow even knew that he and Alegretta had conceived a child. Someone in the clinic had let the news out. But Rafiel took what precautions he could to preserve their privacy. They chose their time – it was after midnight – and the doorwarden reported no one in the area when they stole out and down into the lowest reaches of the arcology.

It turned out that the powerplant wasn't particularly hot. It didn't look dangerous at all; everything was enamelled white or glittering steel, no more worrisome in appearance than a kitchen. It was noisy, though; they both had to put on earplugs when the shift engineer, as a professional courtesy to his colleague, Alegretta, let them in. With all the roaring and whining around them they couldn't talk very well, but Alegretta had explained some of it on the way down, and pointed meaningfully to this great buzzing cylinder and that red-striped blank wall, and Rafiel was nearly sure he understood what he was seeing. He knew it was muon-catalysed fusion. He even knew that it was, in fact, the most desperately desired dream of powerplant designers for generations, a source of power that took its energy from the commonest of all elements: hydrogen, the same universal fuel that stoked the fires of the stars themselves, and delivered it in almost any form anyone could wish – heat, kinetic energy or electricity – without fuss or bother. Well, not entirely without *bother*. It had taken a long time and a lot of clever engineering to figure out how to get the pions to make the muons that would make the reaction go; but there it was. Lukewarm fusion operated without violent explosions, impossible containment or deadly radioactive contamination. It worked best at an optimal temperature of 700 degrees Celsius (instead of many thousands!), and so it was intrinsically both safe and convenient. It was, really, the fundamental reason why the living members of the human race now outnumbered the dead. The foetal procedures could extend life, but it was only the cheap and easy energy that would never run out that could keep all ten trillion human beings alive.

'Thanks,' Alegretta said to the shift engineer as he collected their dosimeters and earplugs on the way out. Rafiel wasn't looking at the engineer as she checked the dosimeters and nodded to Alegretta to show they were all right. He was looking at Alegretta, so small and pretty and, well, yes, so *young* to be the master of so much energy.

And so damned *intelligent*. She was explaining the system to him, pleased and flushed, as they moved toward the exit door. 'It's really hydrogen we burn; it's muonized deuterium; you know, the heavy isotope of hydrogen, but with a muon replacing its electron.'

He didn't know, but he said, 'Yes. Yes, I see.'

She was going right on. 'So, since the muon is heavier, it orbits closer to the nucleus. This means that two atoms of deuterium can come closer to each other than electron-hydrogen ever could, and thus they fuse very easily into helium – oh, *hell*!' she finished, looking out the door. 'Who are *they*?'

He swore softly and took her arm. 'Come on,' he said, pushing their way through the swarm of paparazzi.

*

'We must have been seen going in,' he told her, once they were safely back in the condo. 'Or your friend the engineer called somebody.'

'Is it always like this, Rafiel?'

He wanted to be honest with her. 'Sometimes we tip the paps off ourselves,' he admitted. 'I mean, I don't *personally* do it. I don't have to. Jeftha or Mosay or somebody will, because we *want* the paparazzi there, you know? They're good for business. They're the source of the publicity that makes us into stars.'

'Did you?'

'Did I tip them off? No. No, this time they found us out on their own. They're good at that.'

ₓSo he had no secrets any more: the paparazzi knew that his life was nearing its end and that he had started a child he would not live to see grow, all of which made him more newsworthy than ever, for the same reasons: because he was Rafiel, the short-timer; because he was going to do that black-comic thing, to die. Since hardly anybody really suffered, people like Rafiel filled a necessary niche in the human design: they did the suffering for everyone else to enjoy vicariously – and with the audience's inestimable privilege of turning the suffering off when they chose.

'Yes, but is it *always* like this?'

He picked up the kitten and cradled it in his arms, upside down, its blue eyes looking up warily at him.

'It will be as long as we're here together,' he said.

She did not respond to that. She just walked silently over to the communications screen.

It seemed to Rafiel that his beloved wanted not to be beloved, or not actively beloved, right then. Her back was significantly turned toward him. She had taken some faxes from *Hakluyt* and was poring over them, not looking at him. He took his cue from her and went into the other room to deal with a couple of callbacks. He did not think he had satisfactorily explained the situation to her. On the other hand, he didn't think he had to.

When he came back she was sitting with a fax in her hand, purring Nicolette in her lap, her head down. He stood there for a moment, looking not at Alegretta but at the cat. The little animal showed no sign of the human gene splices that let her be a temporary incubator for their child. She was just a cat. But inside the cat was the child which would see such wonders, for ever denied to himself – a new sun in the sky, planets (*perhaps* planets, anyway) where no human had ever set foot – all the things that were possible to someone with an endless life ahead of him.

He knew that the thing in the cat's belly was not actually a *child* yet, hardly even a real foetus; it was no longer than a grain of dust, but already it was richer in powers and prospects than its father would ever be.

Then, as Alegretta moved, he saw that she was weeping.

He stood staring at her, more embarrassed than he had ever been with Alegretta before. He couldn't remember ever seeing an adult cry before. Not even himself. He moved uncomfortably and must have made some small noise, because she looked up and saw him there.

She beckoned him over and put her hand on his. 'My dear,' she said, still weeping, 'I can't put it off any longer. I have to be there for the final tests, so – I have to leave tomorrow.'

'Come to bed,' he said.

In the morning he was up before her. He woke her with a kiss. She smiled up at him as she opened her eyes, then let the smile slip away as she remembered, finally saw what he was holding in his hand. She looked at him in puzzlement. 'What's that thing for?'

He held up the little cage. 'I sent the server out for it first thing this morning,' he said. 'It's to put the kitten in for the trip. We don't want to break the family up again, do we?'

'We?'

He shrugged. 'The you and me we. I decided I really wanted to see your *Hakluyt* before it takes you away from me.'

'But Rafiel! It's such a long trip to *Hakluyt*!'

'Kosmojets go there, don't they?'

'Of course they do, but' – she hesitated, then plunged on – 'but are you up to that kind of stress, Rafiel? I mean physically? Just to get into orbit is a strain, you know; you have to launch to orbit through the railgun, and that's a seven-gee acceleration. Can you stand seven gees?'

'I can', he said, 'stand anything at all, except losing you so soon.'

12

Rafiel is excited over the trip. Their first leg is an airplane flight. It's his first time in a plane in many years, and there's no choice about it; no maglev trains go to the Peruvian Andes. That's where the railgun is, on the westward slope of a mountain, pointing toward the stars. As the big turboprop settles in to its landing at the base of the railgun, Rafiel gets his first good look at the thing. It looks like a skijump in reverse: its traffic goes up. *The scenery all around is spectacular. Off to the north of the railgun there's a huge waterfall which once was a hydroelectric dam supplying power to half Peru and almost all of Bolivia. Lukewarm-fusion put the hydropower plants out of business and now it is just a decorative cataract. When they get out Rafiel finds his heart pounding and his breath panting, for even the base of the railgun is nearly 2500 metres above sea level, but he doesn't care. He is* thrilled.

While they were dressing in their cushiony railgun suits, Rafiel paused to listen to the scream of a capsule accelerating up the rails to escape velocity. Alegretta stopped what she was doing, too, to look at him. 'Are you *sure* you can handle this?' she asked. His offhand wave said that he was very, very sure. She checked him carefully as he got into each item of the railgun clothes. What they wore was important – no belts for either of them, no brassiere for Alegretta, slippers rather than shoes, no heavy jewellery – because the seven-gee strain would cost them severely for any garment that pressed into their flesh or constrained their freedom. When Alegretta was satisfied about that, she got to the serious problem of fitting baskets to the cats.

'Will she be all right?' Rafiel asked anxiously, looking at Nicolette – meaning, really, will the almost-baby in her belly be all right?

'I'll make her be all right,' Alegretta promised, checking

the resilience of the padding with her knuckles. 'That'll do. Anyway, cats stand high-gee better than people. You've heard stories of them falling out of tenth-storey windows and walking away? They're true – sometimes true, anyway. Now let's get down to the loading platform.'

That was busier than Rafiel had expected. Four or five other passengers were saying good-byes to friends on the platform, but it wasn't just people who were about to be launched into space. There were crates and cartons, all padded, being fitted carefully into place in the cargo section, and servers were strapping down huge Dewars of liquid gas. 'Inside,' a guard commanded, and when they were in the capsule a steward leaned over them to help with the straps and braces. 'Just relax,' he said, 'and don't turn your heads.' Then he bent to check the cat baskets. The kitten was already asleep, but her mother was obviously discontented with what was happening to her. However, there wasn't much she could do about it in the sweater-like restraint garment that held her passive. . . . No, Rafiel thought, not a sweater; more like a straitjacket—

And then they were on their way.

The thrust squeezed all the breath out of Rafiel, who had not fully remembered what seven gees could do to him. The padded seat was memory plastic and it had moulded itself to his body; the restraints were padded; the garments were without wrinkles or seams to cut into his flesh. But still it was *seven gees*. The athletic dancer's body that had never gone over seventy-five kilograms suddenly and bruisingly weighed more than half a ton. Breathing was frighteningly difficult; his chest muscles were not used to expanding his ribcage against such force. When he turned his head, ever so minutely, he was instantly dizzied as the bones of the inner ear protested being twisted so viciously. He thought he was going to vomit; he forced himself to breathe.

It lasted only for a few minutes. Then they were free. The acceleration stopped. The railgun had flung the capsule off its tip, and now they were simply thrown free into the sky, weightless. The only external force acting on the railgun launch capsule now was the dwindling friction of the outside air; that pressed Rafiel's body against the restraining straps at first, but then it, too, was gone.

'Congratulations, dear Rafiel,' said Alegretta, smiling. 'You're in space.'

Once they had transshipped to a spacecraft it was eight days to Mars-orbit, where *Hakluyt* hung waiting for them. There were a few little sleeping cabins in the ship, in addition to the multi-bunk compartments. The cabins were expensive, but that was not a consideration for Rafiel, who was well aware that he had far more money than he would ever live to spend. So he and Alegretta and the cats had their own private space, just the four of them – or five, if you counted the little cluster of cells that was busily dividing in the white cat's belly, getting ready to become a person.

Their transport was a steady-thrust spacecraft, accelerating at a sizeable fraction of a gee all the way to turnaround, and decelerating from then on. It was possible to move around the ship quite easily. It was also pointless, because there was nothing much to do. There was no dining room, no cabaret, no swimming pool on the aft deck, no gym to work out in. The servers brought meals to the passengers where they were. Most of the passengers spent their time viewing vid programmes, old and new, on their personal screens. Or sleeping. In the private cabin Rafiel and Alegretta had several other options, one of which was talking; but even they slept a lot.

More than a lot.

When, at their destination, they were docking with the habitat shuttlecraft Rafiel, puzzled, counted back and realized that he had only slept twice on the trip. They had to have been good long sleeps – two or three full twenty-four-hour days at a time; and that was when he realized that Alegretta had doped him to make him rest as much as possible.

13

On board the Hakluyt, *Alegretta disappears as soon as Rafiel is settled in. She can't wait to see what damage her deputy may have done to her precious engines. This leaves Rafiel free to explore the habitat. There's no thrust on* Hakluyt's *engines yet, just the slow roll of the habitat to distinguish up from down. That's a bit of a problem for everybody. All habitats spin slowly so that centrifugal force will supply some kind of gravity. But when* Hakluyt *starts to move they'll stop the spin because they won't need it any more. The 'down' the spin has provided them – radially outward from the central axis of the cylindrical habitat – will be replaced by a rearward 'down', toward the thruster engines in the stern. Consequently, every last piece of furnishing will have to be rearranged as walls become floors and floors walls. Rafiel is having a lot of trouble with his orientation. Besides the fact that half the fittings have already been relocated, the light-gee pull is strange to him. Because he has spent so little time in low-gee environments he instinctively holds on to things as he walks, though really the feeling isn't much different from being on, say, the Moon. (But Rafiel hasn't been even there for nearly half a century.) Once he gets used to these things, though, he's fascinated. Everything so* busy! *Everyone in such a* hurry! *The whole ship's complement has turned out to finish loading, even small children – Rafiel is fascinated to see how many children there are. Young and old, they can't wait to start on their long interstellar journey – and aren't very patient with people (even very famous people) who happen to get in their way.*

By the time Rafiel had been three days on *Hakluyt* he was beginning to get used to the fact that he didn't see much of Alegretta. Not when she was awake, at least. When she was awake all she seemed to have time for was to check on his vital signs and peer into her computer screen when she'd stuck sensors to his chest and make sure he was taking his spansules. Then she was off again, looking harried.

They did sleep together, of course, or at least they slept in the same bed. Not necessarily at the same times. Once or twice Rafiel came back to their tiny compartment and found her curled up there, out cold. When she felt him crawl in beside her she reached out to him. He was never quite certain she was awake even when they made love – awake enough to respond to him, certainly, and for a few pleased mumbles when they were through, but nothing that was actually articulate speech.

It was almost good enough, anyway, just to know that she was nearby. Not quite; but still it was fascinating to explore the ship, dodging the busy work teams, trying to be helpful when he could, to stay out of the way, at least, when he couldn't. The ship was full of marvels, not least the people who crewed it (busy, serious, plainly dressed and so *purposeful*). A special wonder was the vast central space that was a sort of sky as the habitat rotated (but what purpose would it serve when they were under way?). The greatest wonder of all was *Hakluyt* itself. It was going to go where no human had ever, *ever*, gone before.

Everything about the ship delighted and astonished. Rafiel discovered that the couch in their room became a bed when they wanted it to, and if they didn't want either it disappeared entirely into a wall. There was a keypad in the room that controlled air, heat, lights, clock, messages – might run all of *Hakluyt*, Rafiel was amused to think, if he only knew what buttons to push. Or if all the things worked.

The fact was, they didn't all work. When Rafiel tried to get a news broadcast from Earth the screen produced a children's cartoon, and when he tried to correct it the whole screen dissolved into the snow of static. The water taps – hot, cold, potable – all ran merely cold.

When he woke to find exhausted Alegretta trying to creep silently into their bed, he said, making a joke, 'I hope the navigation system works better than the rest of this stuff.'

She took him seriously. 'I'm sorry,' she said, weary, covetously eyeing the bed. 'It's the powerplant. It wasn't originally designed to drive a ship, only to supply power for domestic needs. Oh, it has plenty of power. But they located the thing midships instead of at the stern, and we had to brace everything against the drive thrust. That means relocating the water reservoirs – don't drink the water, by the way, dear; if you're thirsty, go to one of the kitchens – and— Well, hell,' she finished remorsefully. 'I should have been here.'

Which added fuel to the growing guilt in Rafiel. He took a chance. 'I want to help,' he said.

'How?' she asked immediately – woundingly, just as he had feared she would.

He flinched, but said, 'They're loading more supplies – fresh wing-bean seeds this morning, I hear. At least I can help shift cargo!'

'You can *not*,' she said in sudden alarm. 'That's much too strenuous! I don't want you dying on me!' Then, relenting, she thought for a moment. 'All right. I'll talk to Borretta, he's loadmaster. He'll find something for you – but now, please, let me come to bed.'

Borretta did find something for him. Rafiel became a children's care-giver in one of the ship's nurseries, relieving for active duty the ten-year-old who had previously been charged with supervising the zero-to-three-year-olds.

It was not at all the kind of thing Rafiel had had in mind, but then he hadn't had much of anything very specifically in his mind, because what did *Hakluyt* need with a tap-dancer? But he was actually helping in the effort. (The ten-year-old he relieved was quite useful in bringing sandwiches and drinks to the sweating cargo handlers.) Rafiel found that he liked taking care of babies. Even the changing of diapers was a fairly constructive thing to do. Not exactly aesthetic, no. Extremely repetitious, yes, for the diapers never *stayed* clean. But while he was doing it he thought of the task as prepaying a debt he would owe to whomever, nine months later, would be changing the diapers of his own child.

The ten-year-old was nice enough to teach Rafiel the

technical skills he needed for the work. More than that, he was nice enough to be acceptably impressed when he found out just who Rafiel was. ('But I've seen you on the screen! And you've got a new show coming out – when? *Soon?*') The boy even brought his older brother – a superior and taller version of the same, all of thirteen – around to meet this certified star. When Rafiel had a moment to think of it, between coaxing a two-year-old to take her nap and attempting to burp a younger one, it occurred to him that he was – yes, actually – quite happy. He liked all these strange, dedicated, space-faring people who shared the habitat with him. 'Strange' was a good word for them, though. Unlike all the friends and colleagues he'd spent his life with, these *Hakluyt*ians spoke unornamented English, without loan words, without circumlocutions. They had basically unornamented bodies, too. Their clothes were simply functional, and even the youngest and best-looking wore no jewels.

When Rafiel had pondered over that for a while an explanation suddenly occurred to him. These people simply didn't have time for frills. Astonishing though the thought was, these *immortal* people were in such a hurry to *do* things that, even with eternities before them, they had no time to waste.

The day before *Hakluyt* was to leave, Alegretta somehow stole enough time from her duties to go with Rafiel to the birthing clinic, where they watched the transfer of their almost-child from Nicolette's tiny belly to the more than adequate one of a placid roan mare. It was a surgical spectacle, to be sure, but peaceful rather than gruesome. Even Nicolette did not seem to mind, as long as Alegretta's hand was on her head.

On the way back to their cabin Alegretta was silent. Stranger still, she was dawdling, when always she was in a hurry to get to the work that she had to do.

Rafiel was aware of this, though he was continually distracted by passers-by. The ten-year-old had spread the word of his fame. It seemed that every third person they passed, however busy, at least looked up and nodded or called a friendly greeting to him. After the twentieth or thirtieth exchange Rafiel said, 'Sorry about all this, Alegretta.'

She looked up at him curiously. 'About what? About the fact that they like you? When's this *Oedipus* going to be released?'

'In about a week, I think.'

'In about a week.' It wasn't necessary for her to point out that in a week *Hakluyt* would be six days gone. 'I think a lot of these people are going to want to watch it,' she said, musing. 'They'll be really sorry you aren't here so they can make a fuss over you when it's on.'

Rafiel only nodded, though for some inexplicable reason internally he felt himself swelling with pleasure and pride. Then he bent close to her, puzzled at the low-pitched thing she had said. 'What?'

'I said, you could be here,' Alegretta repeated. 'I mean, if you wanted to. If you didn't mind not going back to the Earth, ever, because – oh, God,' she wailed, 'how can you say "Because you're going to be dead in a few weeks anyway so it doesn't really matter where you are" in a loving way?'

She stopped there, because Rafiel had put a gentle finger to her lips.

'You just did,' he said. 'And of course I'll come along. I was only waiting to be asked.'

14

Fewer than thirty-six hours have passed since Hakluyt's *launch,
but all that time its stern thrusters were hard at their decades-
long work of pushing the ship across interstellar space. By now it
is already some fifteen million kilometres from its near-Martian
orbit and, with every second that passes, Alegretta's lukewarm-
fusion jets are thrusting it several hundred kilometres farther
away. The reactors are performing perfectly. Still, Alegretta can
hardly bear to let the controls and instruments that tell her so
out of her sight. After the pre-launch frenzy,* Hakluyt's *five
thousand pioneers are beginning to catch up on their sleep. So is
Alegretta.*

Rafiel tried to make no noise as he pulled on his robe
and started toward the sanitary, but he could see Alegretta
beginning to stir in her sleep. Safely outside their room he
was more relaxed – at least, *acted* relaxed, nodding brightly
to the people he passed in the hall. It was only when he
was looking in the mirror that the acting stopped and he
let the fatigue and discomfort show in his face. There was
more of it every day now. The body that had served him
for ninety-odd years was wearing out. But, as there was
absolutely nothing to be done about that fact, he put it out
of his mind, showered quickly, dressed in the pink shorts
and flowered tunic that was the closest he had to *Hakluyt*-
style clothing and returned to their room. By then Alegretta
was sitting dazedly on the edge of the bed, watching Nicolette, at the foot of the bed, dutifully licking her kitten.

'You should have slept a little longer,' he said fondly.

She blinked up at him. 'I can't. Anyway' – she paused
for a yawn – 'there's a staff meeting coming up. I ought to
decide what I want to put in for.'

Rafiel gently pushed the cats out of the way and sat down
companionably next to her. They had talked about her

future plans before. He knew that Alegretta would have to be reassigned to some other task for the long trip. Unless something went seriously wrong with the reactors there would be little for her to do there. (And if, most improbably, anything did go seriously wrong with them in the space between the stars, the ship would be in more trouble than its passengers could hope to survive.) 'What kind of job are you looking for?'

'I'm not sure. I've been thinking of food control, maybe,' she said, frowning. 'Or else waste recycling. Which do you think?'

He pretended to take the question seriously. He was aware that both jobs were full-time, hands-on assignments, like air and water control. If any of those vital services failed, the ship would be doomed in a different way. Therefore human crews would be assigned to them all the time the ship was in transit – and for longer still if they found no welcoming planet circling Tau Ceti. But he knew that there was nothing in his background to help Alegretta make a choice, so he said at random: 'Food control sounds like more fun.'

'Do you think so?' She thought that over. 'Maybe it is, sort of, but I'd need a lot of retraining for aeroponics and trace-element management. The waste thing is easier. It's mostly plumbing, and I've got a good head start on that.'

He kissed her. 'Sleep on it,' he advised, getting up.

She looked worriedly up at him, remembering to be a doctor. 'You're the one who should be sleeping more.'

'I've had plenty, and anyway I can't. Manfred will be waiting for me with the babies.'

'Must you? I mean, should you? The boy can handle them by himself, and you look so tired. . . .'

'I'm fine,' he said, trying to reassure the person who knew better than he.

She scolded, 'You're *not* fine! You should be resting.'

He shook his head. 'No, dearest, I really am fine. It's only my body that's sick.'

He hadn't lied to her. He was perfectly capable of helping with the babies, fine in every way – except for the body.

That kept producing its small aches and pains, which would steadily become larger. That didn't matter, though, because they had not reached the point of interfering with tending the children. The work was easier than ever now, with the hectic last-minute labours all completed. The ten-year-old, Manfred Okasa-Pennyweight, had been allowed to return to the job, which meant that now there were two of them on the shift to share the diapering and feeding and playing.

Although Rafiel had been demoted to his assistant, Manfred deferred to him whenever possible. Especially because Manfred had decided that he might like to be a dancer himself – well, only for a *hobby*, he told Rafiel, almost apologizing. He was pretty sure his main work would be in construction, once they had found a planet to construct things on. And he was bursting with eagerness to see Rafiel perform. 'We're all going to watch the *Oedipus*,' he told Rafiel seriously, looking up from the baby he was giving a bottle. 'Everybody is. You're pretty famous here.'

'That's nice,' Rafiel said, touched and pleased, and when there was a momentary break he showed the boy how to do a cramp roll, left and right. The babies watched, interested, though Rafiel did not think it was one of his best performances. 'It's hard to keep your feet down when you're tapping in a quarter-gee environment,' he panted.

Manfred took alarm. 'Don't do any more now, please. You shouldn't push yourself so hard,' he said. Rafiel was glad enough to desist. He showed Manfred some of the less strenuous things, the foot positions that were basic to all ballet . . . though he wondered if ballet would be very interesting in this same environment. The grandest of leaps would fail of being impressive when the very toddlers in the nursery could jump almost as high.

When their shift was over, Manfred had a little time to himself before going to his schooling. Bashfully he asked if Rafiel would like to be shown anything on the ship, and Rafiel seized the chance. 'I'd like to see where they do the waste recycling,' he said promptly.

'You really want to go to the stink room? Well, of course, if you mean it.' And on the way Manfred added chattily, 'It probably doesn't smell too bad right now, because most of the recycled organics now are just chopped-up trees and things – they had to cut them all down before we launched, because they were growing the wrong way, you see?'

Rafiel saw. He smelled the processing stench, too; there was a definite odour in the waste-recycling chambers that wasn't just the piney smell of lumber, though the noise was even worse than the smell. Hammering and welding was going on noisily in the next compartment, where another batch of aeroponics trays were being resited for the new rearward orientation. 'Plants want to grow *upward*, you see,' Manfred explained. 'That's why we had to chop down all those old trees.'

'But you'll plant new ones, I suppose?'

'Oh, I don't think so. I mean, not pines and maples like these. They'll be planting some small ones – they help with the air recycling – and probably some fruit trees, I guess, but not any of these big old species. They wouldn't be fully grown until we got to Tau Ceti, and then they'd just have to come down again.'

Rafiel peered into the digesting room, where the waste was broken down. 'And everything goes into these tanks?'

'Everything organic that we don't want any more,' Manfred said proudly. 'All the waste, and everything that dies.'

'Even people?' Rafiel asked, and was immediately sorry he had. Because of course they had probably never had a human corpse to recycle, so far.

'I've seen enough,' he said, giving the boy a professional smile. He did not want to stay in this place where he would soon enough wind up. He would never make it to Tau Ceti, would never see his son born ... but his body would at some fairly near time go into those reprocessing vats, along with the kitchen waste and the sewage and the bodies of whatever pets died en route, ultimately to be turned into food that would circulate in that closed ecosystem for ever. One way or another, Rafiel would never leave them.

While Alegretta was once again fussing over her diagnostic

readouts Rafiel scrolled the latest batch of his messages from Earth.

The first few had been shocked, incredulous, reproachful; but now everyone he knew seemed at least resigned to their star's wild decision, and Mosay's letters were all but ecstatic. The paps were going crazy with the story of their dying Oedipus going off on his last great adventure. Even Docilia was delighted with the fuss the paps were making, though a little put out that the stories were all *him*, and Alegretta was pleased when the news said that another habitat had been stirred to vote for conversion to a ship; maybe Rafiel's example was going to get still others to follow them.

But she was less pleased with the vital signs readings on her screen. 'You really should go into the sickbay,' she said fretfully.

'So they could do what for me?' he asked, and of course she had no answer to that. There was no longer much that could be done. To change the subject Rafiel picked up the kitten. 'Do you know what's funny here?' he asked. 'These cats. And I've seen dogs and birds – all kinds of pets.'

'Why not? We like pets.' She was only half attentive, most of her concentration on the screen. 'Actually, I may have started the fashion myself.'

'Really? But on Earth most people don't have them. You hardly ever see a pet animal in the arcologies. Aren't you afraid that they'll die on you?'

She turned to look at him, suddenly angry. 'Like you, you mean?' she snapped, her eyes flashing. 'Do you see what the screen is saying about your tests? There's blood in your urine sample, Rafiel!'

For once, he had known that before she did, because he had seen the colour of what had gone into the little flask. He shrugged. 'What do you expect? I guess my *rognons* are just wearing out. But, listen, what did you mean when you said you started the fashion—'

She cut him off. 'Say kidneys when you mean kidneys,' she said harshly, looking helpless and therefore angry because she was helpless. He recognized the look. It was almost the way she had looked when she first gave him the bad news about his mortality, so long and long ago, and it chased his vagrant question out of his mind.

'But I'm still feeling perfectly well,' he said persuasively – and made the mistake of trying to prove it to her by walking a six-tap riff – a slow one, because of the light gravity.

He stopped, short of breath, after a dozen steps.

He looked at her. 'That didn't feel so good,' he panted. 'Maybe I'd better go in after all.'

15

*Hakluyt's sickbay is just about as big as a hospital in an average
Earthly arcology, and just about as efficient. Still, there is a limit
to what any hospital can do for a short-timer nearing the end of
his life expectancy. When, after four days, they wake Rafiel, he
is in far from perfect health. His face is puffy. His skin is sallow.
But he has left strict orders to wake him up so he can be on hand
for the showing of Oedipus. As nothing they can do will make
much difference anyhow, they do as he asks. They even fetch the
clothes he requests from his room, and when he is dressed he looks
at himself in a mirror. He is wearing his fanciest and most
theatrical outfit. It is a sunset-yellow full dress suit, with the
hem of the tails outlined in stitches of luminous red and a
diamond choker around his neck. The diamonds are real. With
any luck at all, he thinks, people will look at his clothing and
not at his face.*

Probably not every one of *Hakluyt*'s five thousand people
were watching *Oedipus* as the pictures beamed from Earth
caught up with the speeding interstellar ship. But those who
were not were in a minority. There were twenty viewers
keeping them company in the room where Rafiel and Alegretta sat hand in hand, along with Manfred and his brother
and a good many people Rafiel didn't really know – but
whom Manfred knew, or Alegretta did, and so they were
invited to share.

It was a nice room. A room that might almost have been
Rafiel's own old condo, open to the great central space
within *Hakluyt*; they could look out and see hundreds of
other lighted rooms like their own, all around the cylinder,
some a quarter of a kilometre away. And most of the people
in them were watching, too. When the four children of
Jocasta and Oedipus did their comic little dance at the
opening of the show, the people in the room laughed where

Mosay wanted them to – and two seconds later along came the distant, delayed laughter from across the open space, amplified enough by the echo-focusing shape of the ship to reach their ears.

Rafiel hardly looked at the screen. He was content simply to sit there, pleased with the success of the show, comfortable with Alegretta's presence . . . at least, in a general sense comfortable; comfortable if you did not count the sometimes acute discomforts of his body. He didn't let the discomforts show. He was fondly aware that Alegretta's fingers slipped from hand to wrist from time to time, and knew that she was checking his pulse.

He was not at all in serious pain. Of course, the pain was there. Only the numbing medications they had been giving him were keeping it down to an inconvenience rather than agony. He accepted that, as he accepted the fact that his life expectancy was now measured in days. Neither fact preyed on his mind. There was an unanswered question somewhere in his mind, something he had wanted to ask Alegretta, but what it could have been he could not clearly say. He accepted the fact that his mind was confused. He even drowsed as he sat there, aware that he was drifting off for periods of time, waking only when there was laughter, or a sympathetic sound from the audience. He did not distinguish clearly between the half-dreams that filled his mind and the scene on the screens. When the audience murmured as he – as Oedipus – took his majestic oath to heal the sickness of the city, the murmur mingled in Rafiel's mind with a blurry vision of the first explorers from *Hakluyt* stepping out of a landing craft on to a green and lovely new planet, to the plaudits of an improbable welcoming committee. It wasn't until almost the end that he woke fully, because next to him there was a soft sound that had no relation to the performance on the screen.

Alegretta was weeping.

He looked at her in confusion, then at the screen. He had lost an hour or more of the performance. The play was now at the farewell of the chorus to the blinded and despair-

ing Oedipus as, alone and disgraced, he went off to a
hopeless future. And the chorus was singing:

> There goes old Oedipus.
> Once he was the best of us.
> Now he drowns in misery and dread.
> Down from the top he is,
> Proof that all happiness
> Can't be known until you're dead.

Rafiel thought that over for some time. Then, blinking
himself awake, he reached to touch Alegretta's cheek. 'But
I do know that now,' he said, 'and, look, I'm not dead yet.'

'Know what, Rafiel?' she asked huskily, not stopping what
she was doing. Which, curiously, was pressing warm, sticky,
metallic things to his temples and throat.

'Oh,' he said, understanding, 'the show's over now, isn't
it?' For they weren't in the viewing room any more. He
knew that, because he was in a bed – in their room? No,
he decided, more likely back in the ship's sickbay. Another
doctor was in the room, too, hunched over a monitor, and
in the doorway Manfred was standing, looking more startled
than grieving, but too grieving to speak.

Rafiel could see that the boy was upset and decided to
say something reassuring, but he drifted off for a moment
while he tried to think of what to say. When he looked
again the boy was gone. So was the other doctor. Only
Alegretta sat beside him, her eyes closed wearily and her
hands folded in her lap; and at that moment Rafiel remembered the question on his mind. 'The cats,' he said.

Alegretta started. Her eyes flew open, guiltily turning to
the monitor before they returned to him. 'What? Oh, the
cats. They're fine, Rafiel. Manfred's been taking care of
them.' Then, looking at the monitor again, 'How do you
feel?'

That struck Rafiel as a sensible question. It took him a
while to answer it, though, because what he felt was almost
nothing at all. There was no pain in the gut, nor anywhere

109

else, only a sort of generalized numbness that made it hard for him to move.

He summed it all up in one word. 'Fine. I feel fine.' Then he paused to rehearse the question that had been on his mind. When it was clear he spoke. 'Alegretta, didn't you say you started the fashion of having pets?'

'Pets? Yes, I was one of the first here on *Hakluyt*, years and years ago.'

'Why?' he asked. And then, because he felt a need to hurry, he made his thickening tongue come out with it: 'Did you do it so you could get used to things you loved dying? Things like me?'

'I didn't know you were a psychotherapist, dear Rafiel,' she whispered. It was an admission, and she knew he understood it . . . though his eyes had closed and she could not tell whether he had heard the words. She did not need the confirmation of the screen or of the other doctor as he came running in to know that Rafiel had joined the minority of the dead. She kissed the unresponding lips and retired to the room they had shared, to weep, and to think of what, some day, she would tell their son about his father: that he had been famous, and loved, and brave . . . and most of all that, certainly, yes, Rafiel had after all been happy in his life, and known that to be true.